PHOENIX MISTRESS

Frank Wadleigh

PHOENIX MISTRESS

This novel is a work of fiction. The characters, names, incidents, dialogue, correspondence, and plot are the products of the author's imagination or are used fictitiously. With the exception of publicly-known figures any resemblance to actual persons or events is purely coincidental.

iUniverse books may be ordered through booksellers or by contacting:

iUniverse
1663 Liberty Drive
Bloomington, IN 47403
www.iuniverse.com
1-800-Authors (1-800-288-4677)

Because of the dynamic nature of the Internet, any web addresses or links contained in this book may have changed since publication and may no longer be valid. The views expressed in this work are solely those of the author and do not necessarily reflect the views of the publisher, and the publisher hereby disclaims any responsibility for them.

Any people depicted in stock imagery provided by Thinkstock are models, and such images are being used for illustrative purposes only.
Certain stock imagery © Thinkstock.

ISBN: 978-1-4917-6424-4 (sc)
ISBN: 978-1-4917-6426-8 (hc)
ISBN: 978-1-4917-6425-1 (e)

Library of Congress Control Number: 2015904980

Print information available on the last page.

iUniverse rev. date: 04/15/2015

DEDICATION

To all who have suffered from the Vietnam War and all wars

An excerpt from a famous 18th century Vietnamese poem where two lovers are parting:

He climbed on his horse, she let go of his gown.
The maple woods were dyed with autumn shades.
He rode off in a cloud of ocher dust
and vanished into the mulberry groves.

She walked back home to face the night alone, and
by himself he fared the distant way.

Who then has cut their moon in two,
One half printing itself on her lonely pillow,
The other lighting the high road?

Nguyen Du
The Story of Kieu

NOTES TO THE READER

To help the reader distinguish fact from fiction in the book:

Fact
The author was Senior Intelligence Analyst in Saigon during the Vietnam War from 1969 to 1971.
Description of Headquarters, MACV, Military Assistance Command, Vietnam
The Hamlet Evaluation System
The Phoenix Program, including congressional investigations and proceedings
Newspaper headlines and articles
Quotes from public figures
Prisons and Vietnamese student anti-war protests
Public places in Saigon: restaurants, nightclubs, hotels, etc.
War-time situation in the mentioned outlying provinces of Saigon
Details of the Viet Cong Infrastructure (VCI)

Fiction
All events, other than those listed above, are fictional.
Although the book is written in first person, the protagonist, and all other persons, with the exception of publicly-known figures, are entirely fictional.

The present tense ('historic present') is sometimes used to show immediacy.

As standard in English language books, Vietnamese diacritical marks are omitted.

PROLOGUE

It was 1969, the year of Ho Chi Minh's death. The attitude of many Americans had turned sharply against the war in Vietnam. This was due to a combination of the 1968 Tet offensive with its garish TV coverage that shocked the country and, later in the year, the making public of the My Lai massacre, one year after the event. The nation was split in two, with anti-war protesters on one side, and President Nixon's so-called "Silent Majority" on the other. Nixon had promised a gradual troop withdrawal, letting the Vietnamese take over the fighting, a program called "Vietnamization."

The American public was not yet aware of a covert CIA operation called the "Phoenix Program" that had been designed to annihilate, or "neutralize" as the CIA put it, the Viet Cong's political apparatus, known as the "Viet Cong Infrastructure" or VCI.

CHAPTER 1

Bored with my routine computer job in the Southern California defense industry, I wanted some adventure in my life and decided to accept an offer as Senior Intelligence Analyst with an American computer company under contract with the US Army in Saigon. It was 1969 and the war in Vietnam was still raging. How would it be to go there as a civilian?

Friends and relatives were shocked at this idea and warned me of the dangers. They would say things like, "Stay out of the Floating Restaurant; they exploded a bomb there recently and a lot of people were killed." I was too intent on changing my life style to let these warnings worry me.

An initial telephone call to the company was followed by a face-to-face interview at a hotel near LAX, the Los Angeles International Airport.

In the lobby I spotted the manager who had come to interview me. He was a tall, tough-looking ex-marine.

"Hi, I'm Mike," he said as he grabbed my hand in a powerful grip. After we had settled into a booth and ordered a couple of beers, he began, "Let me give you some background on what we're doing in Saigon. There is this huge computer program and data management system called the 'Hamlet Evaluation System' or HES. It's run on IBM main frames and is designed to measure government control in hamlets and villages in South Vietnam. It's supposed to show our progress in the war and this information is sent to the military command in Washington and even to the Paris Peace Talks."

"Sounds important," I said.

"Yes it is; that's where your expertise comes in. It seems you have a lot of experience in working with large computer programs."

"Yes, that's right."

"Your assignment will be to work on a revision of this HES program that became necessary after Tet '68, the North Vietnamese/VC offensive. I'm sure you've heard of Tet '68."

"Yes, of course."

"I see from your application that you have never been in the military."

"Yes, I tried to enlist at the beginning of the Korean War, but they refused to take me, on account of a serious problem with my right foot."

Mike nodded and said in a low voice, "Oh, I see."

After the interview questions were out of the way, Mike took a hefty swig of beer and with a big grin said, "You'll love Saigon, the girls are incredible; they say they're among the most beautiful in the world."

"That sounds good!"

"First you'll have to fly to Hawaii for a briefing at our Pacific Headquarters in Honolulu."

"OK, fine," I said.

Well, it really wasn't fine. After a couple of bad flights a few years ago, I had developed an extreme dislike, even fear, of flying. Were there any passenger ships still going to Hawaii? It seemed like a crazy idea. Where to start looking? The yellow pages? Weird! But there actually was an ad for a company called Matson Lines that shipped cars from LA to Honolulu. And they took passengers. I phoned them and booked a cabin. The ship was due to leave in a few days. I would have to tell the company that I was coming by ship. They were quite incredulous, but they accepted it and agreed to pay for it. Great, I didn't have to fly.

The voyage took about seven days. The Pacific Ocean was calm and the food was good. During visits to the bridge, when I told the ship's officers that I was headed to Saigon, they "entertained" me with horror stories of their experiences in Vietnam. These first-hand stories seemed more real than warnings from friends.

The first day of the briefings at the company's Pacific Headquarters in Honolulu, everyone I met was amazed that I had come by ship as no one had ever done that before. When the briefings were finished I was told that I would have to fly to Saigon – no cargo ship for me this time.

The evening of the flight, I went to a party thrown by some people in the company. At about midnight I realized in my inebriated condition that my flight was to leave in one hour. I rushed in my rental car to the freeway, missed the airport exit so then had to make a U-turn, crossing the wide grass median. All I can recall seeing was a mass of car headlights coming towards me. Somehow I merged around and got to the airport, parked the car, and boarded the Pan Am Boeing 707. I was the only civilian; all of the other passengers were military in uniform.

When the stewardess came and asked for my ticket, I was so drunk I couldn't find it in my wallet and kept handing her odd pieces of paper. At stops along the way they kept calling me on the PA system but I was still too drunk to react. I never did find the ticket until I got to Saigon.

Wednesday, December 1, 1969

On arrival at Saigon's huge international Tan Son Nhut airport, a man from the company met me. "Welcome to Vietnam," he said with a sardonic grin, as we shook hands and introduced each other. "I'll be driving you to the company villa where you'll be staying." I was very anxious to see what this place would look like. We drove through the streets of Saigon that were teeming with vehicles of all kinds, military trucks, jeeps, and swarms of two-wheeled traffic spewing out noxious fumes of exhaust. I started to wonder what the hell I was doing here.

About a half hour later we pulled into the driveway of a large, four-story building near the city center. This, I was told, was the company villa, serving as both business office and temporary domicile for new employees until they could find a place to live "on the economy."

The villa looked substantial enough, shaded by luxuriant palm trees that overhung the red-tiled roof. The high branches of tall tamarind trees that lined the adjoining streets were intertwined with each other so that they formed a long, shady tunnel, tropical and beautiful.

The villa was located close to Hai Ba Trung Street, one of Saigon's main thoroughfares, where military trucks competed with streams of Honda motor bikes for ear-splitting decibel levels. The name of the street literally means "Two Trung women," and derives from two famous Vietnamese sister patriots, Trung Trac and Trung Nhi, who fought off Chinese invaders in the first century A.D. and restored independence to their homeland.

Just a block or two away, to the northeast, is the so-called "Plateau," a section of the city that is at a slightly higher elevation than the downtown area. Here are the quiet, tree-shaded residential streets of luxurious villas built by the French during the heyday of colonialism after the First World War.

Checking into the villa, a tall, blonde American secretary in her early twenties gave me a welcoming smile as I introduced myself. "It's nice to see a smiling face," I said, having expected a serious reception in the land where the Vietnam War was being fought. "Oh, we're not all that serious here in the war zone," she replied, laughing. I was feeling better about being here already.

The villa manager showed me to my room on the ground floor, opposite the dining room. It was a lot better than I had expected; a large bedroom with an old-fashioned wardrobe and a bathroom with shower. On the other hand it was an inside room; the two windows gave a view only of the covered entryway. The floor was lined with a gaudy, ornate combination of white and green tiles, giving it a cold, uncomfortable look. The entire villa was air conditioned, something most Americans seemed to require but that I would later learn to live without.

Early next morning, I walked across to the dining room for breakfast where I met the other villa residents. We sat around the long dining table that had places for up to ten people, though it was never full. There were just two other guys living currently at the villa, Ted, a psychologist working on the refugee problem, and Paul, a big, ebullient country boy. Ted was on the short side, wore glasses, and looked to be unconventional. I would later see just how unconventional he could be. Paul was a big guy with crew cut and a look of "everybody's friend." We introduced ourselves and explained our roles in Vietnam.

The two little Vietnamese maids scurried back and forth bringing us eggs, toast, juice, and coffee.

As both of the maids were called "Hue," we named one of them, innovatively, "Hue #1" and the other "Hue #2." Since our tap water was not potable, the maids filled up bottles of boiled and purified water each day. They also did our laundry, washing and scrubbing the clothes in a large concrete trough alongside the walkway leading out to the parking area in front.

After breakfast we climbed into the back of the company Toyota van and headed out into the turmoil of morning traffic. It was amazing

4

how Bien, our Vietnamese driver, could maneuver through the chaotic traffic, dodging motor bikes, pedestrians, and military vehicles during the half-hour drive to my new place of work, Headquarters (HQ), Military Assistance Command, Vietnam (MACV). This enormous complex, nicknamed "Pentagon East," was located on the outskirts of Saigon across the highway from Tan Son Nhut Airport.

Inside the sprawling, two-story MACV ("MACVEE") complex was a bizarre mixture of military personnel in olive drab camouflage jungle fatigues and a relatively small contingent of civilians. The military were dubbed "greenbaggers" by the civilians who, in turn were derisively called "carpetbaggers" by the military. Some said American civilians who volunteered to come to Saigon were "problem people," disappointed in love and running away from it.

Telephones and other communications into and out of HQ were assumed to be monitored by the VC, or "Victor Charlie," and on many phones there was placed a large sticker bearing the warning:

CHARLIE IS LISTENING!

Most of the office space at MACV was sectioned off into small cubicles by means of head-high plastic partitions, the few real offices being reserved for high-ranking officers and upper civilian management. Even some full-bird colonels had to be satisfied with a tiny carrel. The likeness of President Nixon looked down from the walls of the larger offices, including of course the one occupied by General Creighton Abrams, COMUSMACV, Commander, US Military Assistance Command, Vietnam.

I had been assigned to one of these cubicles in the large expanse of offices representing the American pacification program named "Civil Operations and Revolutionary Development Support," or CORDS. The Director of CORDS was William Colby who, as deputy to General Abrams, carried the title "Ambassador," and he was therefore referred to in Saigon as "Ambassador Colby."

Years later, after the war, Colby would become CIA Director back in the States.

In the cubicle next to mine was another civilian, Dave, who had arrived in Saigon the same day as I had. Nearby was an army major and across from me another civilian, Carl, one of the "old-timers" who had been here for four years.

How strange, I thought, to be shut up in these offices while a war was being fought out there.

For the first week I virtually lived in HQ, working evenings and the weekend changing over to the new, revised Hamlet Evaluation System.

The original HES had output overly-optimistic figures of the security status in South Vietnam right up to the 1968 Tet offensive. This had placed the HES in disrepute and there was pressure from the highest levels to make it more accurate and objective.

HES was under attack from both Congress and the press. *The New York Times* headlined:

CONGRESSMAN DISPUTES U.S. ON PACIFICATION GAIN

Representative John V. Tunney, a member of the House Foreign Affairs Committee, charged that the HES figures were overly optimistic.

The HES consisted of 18 questions, organized into six groups under the general categories of security and development. These questions are answered monthly by US military advisers and their Vietnamese counterparts for each of Vietnam's hamlets and villages. A village is a group of, on average, five hamlets. Each hamlet is rated according to a five-point scale ranging from A, the best, with adequate security forces, to E, the worst – VC controlled.

The criteria for evaluation of the hamlets include Viet Cong military activities, subversive political activities, and hamlet defense. The VC subversive political activities concerned the VCI, the VC's "shadow" government which existed often side-by-side with the "legal" Government of Vietnam (GVN).

Commenting later on why he thought we had lost the Vietnam War, Clark Clifford, presidential adviser and McNamara's successor as Secretary of Defense, put it this way:

"Pacification, the program to create a strong government presence in the hamlets and villages of South Vietnam, was generally regarded by American officials as the most important long-term aspect of the war. Our policy failed because it was based on false premises and false promises. If the actual results in Vietnam had approached even remotely what Washington and Saigon had publicly predicted for many years, the American people would have continued to support their government."

The South Vietnamese regime of President Nguyen Van Thieu and Vice-President Nguyen Cao Ky was one of intense political oppression of Buddhists and students. These groups, although mainly non-communist, openly protested against the war and the government. There were the infamous "Tiger Cages" and other prisons. There was torture, a war within a war, carried out under the guise of anti-communism.

The government's use of the so-called "Military Field Tribunal," a kangaroo court where defendants had no representation, was responsible for the sentencing and imprisonment of thousands of persons, denying them the fundamental elements of a fair hearing. Torture and brutality were widespread in the interrogation processes.

The world had recently been watching several cases of political arrest in high government circles. These cases typified the climate of intellectual, religious and political repression that had led to the imprisonment of thousands of loyal Vietnamese nationalists; people who were not pro-communist but simply critical of the Thieu-Ky government were peremptorily arrested, tortured, and imprisoned without trial.

The feeling among the Buddhists was that they had always been discriminated against by the national (Catholic) governments in Saigon. Buddhist students and even some of their professors were singled out by the government for retaliatory acts.

After a peace meeting in September 1968 at Saigon University, the Student Union Building was closed by the police. Students, professors, deputies from the Lower House, and some Buddhist monks had participated in the meeting. Thirty people, mostly students, were arrested.

A medical student at Saigon University was accused of having "leftist tendencies" and was found dead with his hands tied behind his back, having been pushed from a third floor window. The police called it "probable suicide."

The Director of Prisons said that there were 35,000 prisoners in 41 "correctional institutions," and his American advisor estimated that, in addition, there were 10,000 held in interrogation centers, many for up to two years.

An American human rights team investigated prisons in Vietnam at the time and found conditions to be appalling.

They visited the main prisons in Vietnam. The Chi Hoa prison, they reported, was in the form of a hexagon, four stories high, and contained about 5,500 men and boys. Only 40 percent of the inmates had yet been given a trial.

Sometimes prisoners shouted ear-splitting anti-communist slogans. The warden estimated that there were 200 children from 10 to 14 years of age in the prison not yet sentenced.

In one room, about 40 feet by 25 feet, there were 47 children under eight years of age. One child, four years old, said he was in prison because he had been caught stealing a necklace. The children were squatting in one end of the room, eating. The food was rice with vegetables and fish. It looked inadequate. When the warden entered the room, the children immediately left their bowls of food and assembled in lines. All, even the four year old, stood at attention and did not move or speak; only their eyes followed the visitors' moves.

Thu Duc was a prison for women. The cells and large prison rooms were overcrowded. This was especially hard on nursing mothers and those with small children. Fifty women, some with babies, lived in a crude building 40 feet by 30 feet.

On Con Son Island, about 50 miles off the southeast coast, there was an infamous, escape-proof prison, well-known for its so-called "Tiger Cages," small barred cells in which prisoners being disciplined were chained to the floor in a prone position. Con Son contained, according to officials, 7,021 prisoners, most of them "political" who had been "tried" before a Military Field Tribunal, usually without legal representation.

Some of the prisoners were students who had indicated their support for peace and had been arrested during police sweeps of universities.

The prison authorities denied the existence of Tiger Cages. The team was shown two of the prisoners who had been disciplined. They had been in solitary for six months because of their refusal to salute the flag. One said he would never salute it. His legs were deeply marked. The colonel in charge explained that this was the result of a past disease. Questioned directly, the prisoner said it was the result of a long period in leg irons.

Many prisoners were stuffed into small cells which did not allow for lying down or even for sitting, and this, when it was steaming hot and excrement accumulated. Beating by wooden sticks and clubs was the most common form of abuse. The blows were applied to the back and to the bony parts of the legs, to the hands and, in a particularly painful form, to the elevated soles of the feet when the body was in a prone position. Beating of the genitals also occurred. The team also described the immersion of prisoners into tanks of water which were then beaten with a stick on the outside. The pain was said to be particularly intense and the resultant injuries were internal.

Another type of water torture in which a soaked cloth was placed over the nose and mouth of a prisoner, tied back-down to a bench, was said to be very common. The cloth was removed at the last moment before the victim choked to death and then was reapplied. In a related form, water was pumped into the nose.

The most common procedure was said to be the elevation of the victim on a rope bound to his hands which were crossed behind his back. One witness described a "bicycle torture" used in this center. For about a week the prisoner was forced to maintain a squatting position with an iron bar locking his wrists to his ankles. Afterwards he could not walk or even straighten up, it was said. Sexual torture was common, the team reported. Frequently, coke and beer bottles were prodded into the vagina. Also there were a number of accounts of electrical wires applied to the genitals of males and females. Another informant told of the torture by electricity of an eight-year old girl for the purpose of finding her father. This was said to have occurred in the National Police Interrogation Center in Saigon during 1968. Students with notations in their files that they had exhibited "left-wing tendencies" were incarcerated in national prisons and classified as "communists."

At the time I knew nothing about this.

On those evenings after dinner when I didn't go downtown bar-hopping, I would walk up the stairs to the villa roof, a large, flat deck, covered overhead by sheets of translucent-green, corrugated plastic to deflect the torrential monsoon rains. A small refrigerator sat behind the bar of bamboo where the villa residents gathered to drink beer (mostly it was *Black Label*) in the evening hours after work. A notice posted next to the fridge pleaded with beer drinkers:

The only means of supply for beer is with your personal ration card so please cooperate in buying your share.

From our rooftop vantage point at night, those of us living in the villa could see in the distance bright flares slowly parachuting down, providing helicopter gunships and spotters with a view of the Viet Cong. The war was this close yet at the same time seemed very far away.

While Mark Twain was writing *The Adventures of Huckleberry Finn*, the Vietnamese were already fighting the French in Indochina. A representative of the French colonial government was sent to report on the conflict.

How much of what he reported and experienced was condemned to be repeated by the US nearly a century later? If our leaders had only studied their history!

His reports represent a valuable historical document. They first appeared in French in the *Bulletin de la Société des Etudes Indochinoises,* in 1949, and paint a remarkable portrait of the frustrations incurred by the French.

Saigon, 10 August 1883
It seems that we occupy Hai Phong, Hanoi, Nam Dinh and four or five other places but in reality control only the areas that are within range of our guns.

The general opinion is that we must bombard Hue immediately. But Paris has refused us the authority to do this under the pretext that war has not been declared.

However, this may be circumvented; the orders have been given to send troops and, if the ultimatum is not met, to march on Hue. All of us hope that France will not abandon us as that would be a real disaster.

10 October 1883

Everyone here is very upset and indignant after reading in the Saigon papers that there is a mood of reconciliation in France, that a conference will be held in London, that we will give up almost half of Tonkin. We don't want to believe all that for it would be too big a retreat. How can they reconcile this with the treaty of Hue? We await explanation and, having no telegraph, our leaders cannot make a move without fear of disagreement with the French government.

He had some interesting observations on life in Saigon that were not unique to that time.

Saigon is the city of gossip par excellence. People gossip about everything and everybody. The civil servants, since they have nothing much to do, pass the time of day looking for lice in each other's hair. But it is especially the wives of these men who tear at each other. No one is spared and I don't think an honest woman could stay here long without having her reputation tarnished somehow by one of her good friends. Also, the anonymous letter is often received, I hear. All this comes from jealousies of clothing, vehicles, but especially about the status and advancement of their husbands.

For the past week it has rained everyday, but usually the rainstorms that batter Saigon come between 5 and 6 in the evening and last for no more than an hour. The rain, though very warm, refreshes temporarily the air but the humidity is excessive and everything made of leather gets covered with a greenish mold and anything metal quickly rusts.

Ants and mosquitoes are two of the greatest nuisances in Cochinchina. Against the first, there are, unfortunately, few remedies and some of us have had the misfortune of finding myriads in our bed. To protect against mosquitoes we have mosquito nets which are adequate if you take the precaution to close them carefully on the bed as soon as day begins to lower, and then the geckos take on the serious task of chasing them. These animals, small, yellow lizards between 6 and 7 centimeters in length, promenade along the walls and on the ceiling without a care for the laws of gravity. They run very fast and gobble up mosquitoes as soon as they land on the wall. They are respected by everyone for the services they render. Sometimes one sees 10 or 20 on the same wall.

Roger, our secretary at MACV, announced to us in the office that he was going to give a party at his apartment in one of the posh residential regions of the capital.

Roger was an intellectual type, spoke French and played classical music on the piano. He said he had come to Saigon to "escape Muzak." I usually did not like parties but decided to go and check out what there was here in the way of available females.

To get to the party, I decided to borrow a bicycle from one of the Vietnamese men working at the villa. I was thinking of buying one and wanted to see how it was to ride a bike in Saigon. It would be good transportation on my days off. Saigon is relatively flat so is a good "bike city."

There was an odd assortment of people at the party, friends of Roger's from MACV, the American Embassy, and USAID, the United States Agency for International Development. Pronounced "Youse-aid," this was a federal agency responsible for administering civilian foreign aid. They had comfortable facilities, including good restaurants.

After milling around uncomfortably among groups of people I didn't know, I spotted a gal who looked friendly and sauntered up to her. Her name was Angie. We started with the usual small talk. "Why did you come to Saigon?" was a favorite question. Roger, seeing the two of us talking together, came over and, with a mischievous smile, said, "Take a look at this," and handed us a large book with explicit sketches and drawings of couples in various erotic positions. We were pretty surprised at this strange ploy on Roger's part. As we perused the drawings together, we laughed and also were, of course, getting aroused, or "quivering with lust," as Roger told me later the next day. After looking at a number of these provocative scenes, Angie said, a bit timidly, "It's getting late, I really should be going home."

"I would offer to escort you," I said. "The only problem is that I came here by bicycle."

"That's OK," she said, laughing. "I don't live far away. I can take a taxi and you can ride your bike and we'll meet there."

"OK, what's your address?" She wrote it down on the paper napkin from under her drink and handed it to me.

We walked out to the street together and hailed one of the ever-present little Renault blue and white Saigon taxis. As she got into the taxi, I called to her, "I'll see you there." We both headed towards her apartment in downtown Saigon on Le Loi Street, she in a taxi and me following on my bike.

Weaving between cars, I was able to keep up with the taxi and we arrived at the same time. As soon as we entered her apartment she led the way in a fast walk through the lounge into the bedroom. She was not slim by any means, some would have politely said "rotund," but, as with many overweight women, she had a plentiful supply of healthy lust. The drinks and atmosphere of the party, not to mention the effect of the erotic book, had overcome any inhibitions and made the usual foreplay totally unnecessary. It was a purely physical encounter.

Afterwards, I gazed up at the slowly-turning blades of the ceiling fan. The second hand of the clock on the dresser was also revolving, as were the wheels of vehicles that I could hear in Le Loi Street below. For some reason, perhaps now being in the Far East, the idea of Buddhism and its symbol of a wheel came to my mind. Temporarily it was possible to forget that I was in Vietnam and there was a war going on.

From the bed I could hear the chatter of Vietnamese voices in the street below, though they of course had no idea of my existence in that room. I felt myself in a sense both public and private; no one could detect my presence, I was in nearly total secrecy. The French writer Marguerite Duras, commenting on her novel *The Lover*, had said, "There is something of the art of writing in this, the invisibility of the writer in favor of what is written."

I suddenly realized that it was way past the 1:00 a.m. curfew in Saigon when no one is allowed in the streets. We quickly embraced. "Be careful," she whispered. I jumped out of bed, ran down the stairs into Le Loi, unlocked the bike, and rode as fast as I could, hoping to avoid an MP jeep patrol over my violation of the curfew. Tu Do Street was incredibly dark and quiet, not the bright, gaudy strip of shops and girlie bars where I had been with the guys a few nights ago. I rode past the old Continental Palace Hotel, the twin-spired cathedral, and up Nguyen Du Street to the villa. It was very late when I hit the sack; in a few hours I would have to wake up and get out to MACV. But for now it felt good to replay the evening's events. Would this turn out to be just a one-night stand?

CHAPTER 2

Tuesday, December 15

In the morning, Miller, our group leader, came over to my desk. Miller was not too much on my wavelength, a bit older and kind of righteous regarding petty office rules and regulations. He was, however, the group leader so I had to put up with him.

"I have some interesting news for you. Colby wants you to work on the Phoenix program."

"Oh? What sort of work?"

"Colby's office will brief you on it." This was the sort of rigid, short answer I expected from him. He simply walked away without further discussion.

I was intrigued; I had been hearing about this Phoenix program but had not anticipated working on it. It was a bit strange, I thought, to be working for MACV and now becoming involved in a CIA operation. These two agencies had been notorious for their radically conflicting reports on the progress of the war. MACV claimed that we were winning the war by the numbers, while the CIA maintained that one had to include not only the numbers of actual military personnel, but the guerillas as well. There would later be the case of General (William) Westmoreland and "body counts" in the infamous CBS documentary, *The Uncounted Enemy: A Vietnam Deception*, where it was alleged that US military leaders in South Vietnam had discounted the size of the enemy in their reports. The documentary also charged that intelligence officers had purged government databases to hide the deception.

A meeting with Ambassador Colby was arranged. I went to his office, checking in with an administrative assistant, an attractive and intelligent young woman with sparkling eyes. I thought one day I might ask her out. But now was not the time.

Colby was not a tall man and did not have the tough look of someone who, as a former OSS agent, had parachuted behind enemy lines in World War II France. He was, rather, a kind and intelligent-looking person. He welcomed me into his large office and motioned for me to take a seat. After preliminaries, he entered into details of what my assignment would be.

"In Vietnam," he said, "there is a secret communist network within the society that tries to impose its authority on the people through terrorism and threat. This network is called the VC Infrastructure or VCI. It provides the political direction and control of the enemy's war within the villages and hamlets. It lays down the caches for the troops coming from the border sanctuaries; it provides the guides and intelligence for the North Vietnamese strangers; it conscripts, taxes and terrorizes.

"During 1969, over 6,000 people have been killed in terrorist incidents and over 1,200 in assassinations. To fight the war on this level, the government developed a program called Phung Hoang, or Phoenix. It secures information about the enemy organization, identifies the individuals who make it up, and conducts operations against them. This program was formed to bring together the police, the military, and the other government organizations to fight this enemy infrastructure."

"Yes, I've heard about this," I said.

"Since security is so much a part of pacification, it was decided, as you know, to set up an agency called *Civil Operations and Revolutionary Development Support,* or CORDS.

"CORDS has teams at the national, regional, provincial, and district levels. It is a part of the military command structure, in Saigon under General Abrams, and in each of the Corps zones it is under the senior US military commander."

"What is the size of the VCI now?" I asked.

"Our current estimate is about 75,000, but nobody knows yet exactly how many VCI are running this shadow government."

"Is there a quota each year under the Phoenix program?"

"Yes, the quota last year was 1,800 a month. By looking at the documents on the bodies, we can discover frequently that an individual was the head of a district committee or the local security officer for the village committee, or whatever.

"The government has defined the different levels of participation in the Vietcong political effort. This identifies three levels of participation, called A, B, and C.

"The A levels are People's Revolutionary Party Members who have gone through the candidate stage and become convinced members of the enemy apparatus.

"The B levels are leaders of the various front groups, although they may not be party members yet.

"The C levels are generally the rest of the people who participate in the actions.

"You can use the same statistical technique that you are now using on the HES to categorize VCI operatives into A, B, or C classifications depending on their positions in the VCI hierarchy," he explained. "In addition, the HES will have to be modified to better reflect the terrorist activities of the VCI."

"Yes, I understand," I said.

"This is a very professional covert operation that the enemy is running. A normal member of the VCI will have several aliases; he will have all the paraphernalia of covert operations, cutouts, and all that sort of thing. The Phoenix program is aimed at identifying by name the people who do these different jobs so they can be identified and individually picked up."

"How do you identify the people who are active in the infrastructure?" I asked.

"You develop card records on people in the area. Now, initially a number of these reports may be just a single alias, then through the gathering of additional information, you find out that this man's name is really Nguyen Van Thanh or something, and that he was born in a certain section and place.

"You should get familiar with the Phung Hoang Management Information System, or PHMIS. Our computer people can help you with that. It contains data on VC and on VCI. You should also see the Director of National Police. They are responsible for tracking, arresting, and interrogating suspected VC.

"For VCI detainees, there is an arrest report which is in machine-compatible form. This is completed by the National Police (NP) agency making the arrest. There is a so-called *Green Book*, detailing current breakout of VCI executive and significant cadre.

"There is another MACV computer system called VCINS, Viet Cong Infrastructure Neutralization System, that edits data and produces reports on the VCI. On the punched IBM cards there is a column for the individual's name and, in addition to other data, a column for his classification.

"First you will have to do some homework – untangle and understand the complex structure of the Central Office of South Vietnam (COSVN) and the VCI.

"And then you'll need to go out into the Field, to several provinces to find out what is going on in reality and check it against what is being reported. We can arrange your trip in about a week.

"I'd first like you to visit the training program for the RD Cadre, the Revolutionary Development Cadre. These are the guys who actually go out and try to protect the hamlets. The training camp is in Vung Tau. You may also learn something about the so-called Provincial Reconnaissance Units or PRUs."

"Quite a big assignment," I said, smiling. He smiled back with a nod, then asked me if I had any questions. I said that I will certainly have some later.

He concluded with, "My staff will supply you with the material to get started." He got up from his chair – the meeting was obviously over. I thanked him, and said it was an interesting task. As we shook hands, he smiled and said, "Good luck."

The next Sunday I woke up about 7:30, a luxury compared to work days. I was anxious to explore Saigon and have a moment of relaxation before I set off on my new assignment for Colby.

I had my usual breakfast of two fried eggs, toast, fruit juice, and coffee. There were now six of us living at the villa and I was the only one working at HQ MACV; the rest were on other contracts in downtown Saigon or at Tan Son Nhut Airport with the 7th Air Force. My other villa-mates had left earlier that morning but a manager from Hawaii was there and we chatted about the war and what it was like to be living in Hawaii. In the morning those of us living at the villa had to sign up for dinner since the cooks did not want to prepare more food than necessary. If you forgot to sign up in your rush to get to work in the morning, you had to go without dinner – unless of course you were lucky and there were still some leftovers.

After breakfast I walked to Thong Nhut Boulevard near the corner of Mac Dinh Chi in the area of the British and American Embassies. I heard some organ music from St. Christopher's Anglican-Episcopal Church. Under the name *Église Réformée de Saigon,* it conducted services in French at 9:30 on Sunday mornings.

The big wrought iron gates of the outside wall were open so I walked in and wandered around the church courtyard, plush with tropical foliage.

The main doors to the church itself were also wide open and I could see the rows of dark-stained wooden benches or pews. The altar was simple, a little wooden pulpit and some tall, green potted plants in the archway behind it. I went inside and sat on one of the pews near the back. I was the lone person there except for the little Vietnamese caretaker who was now flipping the switch to start the overhead fans – 9:30 was nearing and the morning service, which was to be in French, seemed about to begin. It was a beautiful day, sunny, warm, and breezy with a briskness in the air. Looking out the window I could see that people were just beginning to arrive. The pastor himself, dressed in a long, black robe, was making his way into the church. The shutters had been thrown open and folded back against the inside wall. Everything was showered with sunshine and birds were chirping in the tall trees. A few more people started to amble in from the rectory next door, a stately, ambassadorial villa with high, white-stuccoed walls, and rust-colored roof tiles. The steps and balconies were covered in potted plants.

The pastor began speaking in French. The organ rumbled in a slow, heavy tempo, like a sad funeral procession – the death toll for French influence here, I thought. The pastor stood reading aloud, hands clasped behind his back, rocking forward on the balls of his feet, alternately looking down at his notes, then up to the congregation. His baritone voice matched his stark countenance and close-cut hair. The French words clipped off his lips and echoed in the rotund arches. Outdoors, protected from the blazing sun, were cool, shaded enclaves of tropical foliage. The dark comfort of indoors was accented by rays of bright sunlight piercing through the windows.

Suddenly from outdoors came the deafening sound of an air horn from a big Army truck: "Get the hell out of the way – troops coming through!" Deuce and a halfs (two-and-a-half-ton army trucks) roaring down Thong Nhut Street. Lots of noise – makes it hard to understand the prayers. The insensitivity of life outside.

Next door in the rectory, figures could be seen scurrying about setting table and preparing lunch. One could see through the louvered windows of the rectory to more greenery, yellow with sunlight.

When the service was finally over, the congregation, having purged themselves, could now look forward to earthly pleasures of food. Among the scattered congregation still sitting in the pews was a little girl alone, wearing special shoes – polio. In the next row sat a little boy in shorts, a few older women, and a young man wearing a tie.

I went up and introduced myself to the pastor and then together we walked over to the rectory. There I met his wife who was Vietnamese and pregnant. She spoke excellent French. The pastor was from Normandy and had been in Indochina for the past eleven years except for 1968 when a Swiss pastor and family had substituted for him. Things apparently had been pretty "hairy" during the Tet '68 offensive as they had been caught between the VC firing out of the windows of the US embassy and an ARVN (Army of the Republic of Vietnam) post on the opposite side.

He showed me photos of the church where he had been pastor in Dalat, in the Central Highlands. The little church had been attacked by mortars and machine guns as the VC used it for a base to fire at a military camp nearby. I thanked them for their hospitality and walked back to my room. I was looking forward to a beer at a local bar.

The next day Roger invited me and some of his friends to see the performance of classical Vietnamese dancing and singing at the local *Dai-Nam Theater* sponsored by the President's wife, Madame Thieu. Roger seemed to know a lot of people in Saigon including many VIPs. He was a cool, smooth talker, and cultivated these friendships.

The Vietnamese, though known as poetry lovers, are also enthusiastic for the theater. There is perhaps no better showcase for the lives and loves, the history and cultural heritage, frailties, and traditions of the Vietnamese. For discernible beneath the painted faces, gaudy costumes, props, and the conventional romanticism of the plays are the unchanging moral values of the people, including a generation born and reared in the turmoil of war.

As we were walking towards the theater from our car we heard sirens screaming down the cross street.

"Ha! The theater's probably on fire," I joked. Then we saw the fire engines. "The theater IS on fire," someone shouted. Three fire engines – dilapidated and antique – pulled up to the well-lit theater, completely blocking the street. The little Vietnamese firemen in their shiny chrome Kaiser Wilhelm helmets were scurrying about as in a farce, tugging at and trying to untangle the old fire hoses.

They eventually managed to drag the hoses past the big crowd of well-dressed men and women waiting to get into the theater. As the hoses started to fill with water they sprouted dozens of leaks. Some of the women in high heels had to trot backwards to escape being tripped up by the hoses that were now stretched taut by water pressure. They looked like those little birds at the seashore that scurry back up the beach just ahead of an advancing wave. Some French people behind us in the crowd were jabbering away, wondering whether the performance would be called off. "On a payé!" (We've paid!) declared one of the Frenchmen in a loud voice. In a few minutes, the water was shut off and everyone carefully stepped over the hoses and made their way into the theater where the smoke from the fire made them start coughing and choking. The fire had burned a large hole in the wall high above the stage and a long ladder had been placed there so it could be reached with the fire hose. The theater was crowded with firemen and also QC (Quan Canh, the Vietnamese Military Police) in uniform. One woman said she thought it may have been sabotage. "They told us not to go to these official functions." I learned later that this had been caused by a large bomb placed on a seat in the balcony of the theater.

Was this an attempt on Madame Thieu's life? Eventually the show did go on, but during a musical number, as the singer was at the top of her voice, the firemen switched the searchlight on the big hole in the wall and the audience looked up to see if it was on fire again. The first group of women singers was so amateurish the audience was giggling and looking at each other in disbelief. Madame Thieu never did show up, cautioned about possible sabotage, or perhaps put off by the reviews? The best part of the evening was a color film of *Kim Van Kieu*, a famous Vietnamese epic poem and play, which, to add further absurdity, was accidentally interrupted by a film of a belly dancer in a bar with music blaring out of a juke box. That was the last straw – we decided to leave.

The program, as was customary for these cultural events, was printed in English, Vietnamese, and French, and contained the following intriguing advertisement for a famous Saigon café:

En ces temps difficiles
restez optimistes
Rendez-vous
Chez B R O D A R D
dans son nouveau
Salon de Thé "MEZZANINE"
Vous y verrez la vie en rose

"In these difficult times, stay optimistic; rendez-vous at Brodard in its new tea salon Mezzanine. You will see life through rose-colored glasses."

The next evening after work and dinner I wandered over to Dakao, a quaint little area of Saigon, only about five blocks on each side.

Several bars were the main attractions, as well as two of the best French restaurants in Saigon: *La Cigale* and *Le Lido*. An ad for *La Cigale* appeared in local French newspapers:

La Cigale,

18, Rue Dinh-Tien-Hoang (ex Albert 1er) Dakao
Un coin de France à Saigon
Le rendez-vous des 'Fines Gueules'

Dakao was a well-kept secret – a little place that only insiders knew. It was a picturesque section of the city with little sidewalk food stalls that could be folded up and wheeled away or, even more temporary, food and drinks in the large baskets that women carried on each end of a long, flat bamboo pole. It was amusing to see them carry these weights on each end of a yoke balanced on their shoulders. They had to walk at just the right pace to let the flexing of the pole work for them, not against them. It's something like learning to ride a horse where one has to bounce up and down in a rhythmic way. I looked again at the straw woven baskets bobbing up and down in off-setting rhythm. Vietnam, I thought, interesting – these balancing baskets – a country so out of balance. The statistics, the papers, when they are piled in one basket, what do they equal in the other? I pictured the baskets full of computer printouts.

In the late evening a wonderful aroma of French baguettes from the bakery freshened the air. In earlier times, in the gap between the war with the French and the present one, Dakao was included in tourist attractions for "Saigon by Night" itineraries.

Probably the most popular of the bars in Dakao was *Flora's*, situated prominently on the corner of Dakao's two main streets, Phan Thanh Gian and Dinh Tien Hoang.

By any standards, *Flora's* ranked highest among the bars in Dakao. At the other end of the scale was the *Green Light Bar*, also called *"Ly's Bar"* after the girl of that name who had become very upset when I avoided buying "Saigon tea" by pretending not to understand her. Saigon tea was the fake alcoholic drink that Saigon bar hostesses tried to get GIs and civilians to buy for them. You paid the price for a real alcoholic drink but it was just tea or some other cheap drink, not the alcohol that the men hoped would enable them to seduce the girls.

As you entered *Flora's*, there was a long bar with the usual mirror behind it on the right hand side, and on the left side of the room were the booths. There was a mysterious "upstairs" where occasionally a privileged customer or client would be allowed to go with his girl. The jukebox sat between the long bar and the front window. The one in Flora's was unique; it was quite amusing to listen to "Frosty the Snowman" during evenings when the temperature in Saigon was in the 90's.

Next day I took one of the small, blue and white Renault taxis to Tu Do Street in the main downtown area, where I strolled along looking in the shop windows. Running from the cathedral down to the river past blocks of fashionable shops and sidewalk cafés, Tu Do (Freedom) Street was Saigon's main boulevard. It has been said that Tu Do leads directly from the symbol of religion to that of trade, symbolic of France's early involvement in Indochina.

Tu Do is the most famous of Saigon's thoroughfares and was in French colonial times named "Rue Catinat" after Nicolas Catinat (1637-1712), a marshal of France.

On this street one finds the French style jewelry shops, book stores, cafés, then past Lam Son Square, the Indian-run black market, and the bars, with mini-skirted girls standing in the doorways.

Monsieur Franchini's *Hotel Continental Palace*, situated prominently on Tu Do, is a landmark reminiscent of Graham Greene's *The Quiet American*.

As one descends Tu Do one finally comes to the docks, the *My Canh Floating Restaurant*, and the *Club Nautique*, the French yacht club.

Another aspect of Tu Do Street worth mentioning is that it used to be an "information" center dubbed "Radio Catinat" in the days of the French. The area was the source of rumors which were spread among wealthy businessmen and so-called living-room politicians whose "broadcasting stations" were the numerous bars and restaurants along the street. These rumors usually gave birth to all kinds of speculations on the war or the economic situation, and lots of other 'confidential' news stories.

For a long time after most street names had been changed from French to Vietnamese,

Tu Do continued to be labeled on maps of Saigon by the resonant-sounding "Ex-Catinat." Just to pronounce the old French street names would evoke the colonial past in Saigon.

Tran van Trach, a well-known Vietnamese musician, was so impressed by this particular atmosphere that he composed a song entitled *"Midnight on Catinat Street,"* dedicated to those young lovers who find in Freedom Street an ideal place for their rendezvous at night.

The French magazine *Paris Match* described this street in romantic terms:

Rue Catinat! How many memories! Today it has romantic, shaded places, and its Parisian shop windows: the Portail bookshop, Micheline fashion, the hairdresser Ginette and that bakery Brodard where, on Sunday, after high mass in the cathedral, one goes to buy a Saint-Honoré. The Municipal Theater

has become the Parliament Building. But the old Continental is still there with its imitation Café de la Paix look, its terrace open to the warm night and its little tables with pink lamp shades where it's so good to linger after dinner listening to Viennese waltzes. The enchantment of Saigon. Old colonial houses with their old-fashioned salons where the blades of ceiling fans still turn and, under palm trees, the gardens smelling of snakes and the jungle.

The River Cradles of Civilizations: The Mekong, by Georges Reyer, Paris Match, December, 1961, by permission.

I continued on down Tu Do towards the Saigon River and found a book store, but then realized I had no Piasters to make a purchase. The local currency in Vietnam was the Piaster, referred to by Americans as "P." I spotted a beckoning money changer. The man motioned to me, saying in a low voice, "You want change money?" We withdrew into the shadows for the illegal transaction. The small man counted out the bills for me to see and then rolled them up tight, snapping a rubber band around the package. I handed him the hundred dollars in "green" (US paper money). As I walked away I tried to undo the rubber band but it was so tight that it took me several minutes before I could manage it, discovering to my dismay that only the outer bill was worth anything; the guy had switched rolls in the palm of his hand.

I walked over to the big market. A couple of boys pestered me for a handout. I waved them a goodbye, palm down, but later realized that in Vietnam (and many other places, especially in the East), the signal when you want someone to come to you is to make a motion with the hand, palm down, curling the fingers towards you so that I was actually telling them to come here.

From an article in *The Saigon Post* on Vietnamese customs:

Whatever you do, be careful on how you use your hand in motioning someone toward you. You're sure to get a dirty look or worse if you hold your palm up and wriggle your fingers in signaling to someone. The sign is ordinarily used in Vietnam to attract the attention of dogs and children. However, if you make the same sign but hold your hand flat palm down, nobody will take offense.

As Mike had said in the interview, Vietnamese women were often very beautiful.

A Vietnamese National Tourist Office flyer put it this way:

Perhaps the first thing that strikes foreign visitors when they set foot in the country is the loveliness of the Vietnamese women, often dressed in black slacks and long, white slit tops – the ensemble called "ao dai," pronounced "ao yai" in the south, but "ao zai" in the north. According to many tourists, the ao dai is unique in the world in that it is sexy without being vulgar. The close-fitting bodice, long flowing slit-sided tunic worn with the pantaloons are, according to old-timers, regrettably getting tighter in the leg and losing their inherent allure and grace that is the charm of the Vietnamese feminine attire.

And from *Paris Match*:

They are ravissantes, with doll-like coquetry; they walk by in two's or three's holding each other by the little finger while chattering in the language of birds. They pass by on old velobikes, all flowing robes; one pedaling with her companion, sitting side-saddle behind her. These are the ladies of Saigon, 'Saigon la Française,' the most voluptuous of all the cities of Asia.

I walked down to the Saigon River to see the ships. Saigon is the most important harbor of the Indochinese Peninsula and is one of the rare sea ports in the world where ocean liners have to travel miles up river in order to reach the docks. Nowadays, the vegetation along the banks has been leveled so as to deny cover to the Viet Cong; but in former times, ships passed between banks lined with mangroves, water-palm trees, and rice fields. Sampans and river junks filled with rice, fish, sand, or wood were guided by men using poles or oars. Ships from many countries still call at Saigon: *Messageries Maritimes, American President Lines, Chargeurs-Réunis, Maersk Lines, States Lines, Pacific Far East Line* ("Monthly service from California Ports"), and many others.

In Lam Son Square, a center of Saigon, stands the former Municipal Theater and Opera – now the National Assembly Building. This Saigon landmark has witnessed many historical events. It was built by the French at the end of the nineteenth century. It had 800 seats and every year from

October to May opened its doors to itinerant French dramatic companies. The building was the scene of many Buddhist demonstrations that led to the downfall of the Ngo family regime in November, 1963. It lies between the old, musty Continental Palace Hotel with its slow, often immobilized, French-type iron cage elevators and, facing it across the square, the relatively modern *Hotel Caravelle*.

From the National Assembly Building runs Le Loi Street with its sidewalk stalls that sell everything, including black market goods from the PX. Le Loi leads to the large, covered Central Market and then via Tran Hung Dao Boulevard to Cholon, the Chinese sister city of Saigon.

In 1420 AD, Emperor Le Loi and his army ambushed and defeated a Chinese army of 120,000 soldiers and cavalry. After this great victory, Le Loi changed his country's name to Dai Viet (Greater Viet) and chose Hanoi as its capital.

Crossing Le Loi at right angles is Nguyen Hue Boulevard, which runs from the palatial City Hall on Le Thanh Ton Street, straight down to the Saigon River. The City Hall, built in 1906-1908, is fascinating architecturally with its mansard roofs, arched windows, balconies, and tower.

Nguyen Hue Boulevard is known as the "street of flowers" because of its flower stalls and kiosks that line the median of the Boulevard. It is named after a national hero of the 18th century who became immortal in the minds of the Vietnamese people with his victory over the Chinese invaders.

One of the longest avenues of Saigon is named after Le Thanh Ton, the fourth king of the Le dynasty. During his 38-year reign (1460-1497), Le Thanh Ton defeated the Cham and Lao armies, promulgated new laws, reformed the administrative machinery, built dikes, promoted agriculture, and developed education.

In 1969 the French presence in Saigon was still very strong and there were many newspaper ads for French restaurants, cafés, hotels, nightclubs, cinemas, shops, and associations in the main French language newspapers, *Le Journal d'Extrême-Orient* and *Les Nouvelles du Dimanche*. They are even advertised in the local English language newspapers, *The Saigon Post, The Vietnam Guardian*, and *The Vietnam Sunday Mirror*.

The Saigon Post, selling for 20 Piasters, had ads for villas, rooms for rent, and "friends":

Villa:
Large and comfortable
villa for rent.
Apply 314/4 Phan Thanh Gian Saigon

In a separate ad:

Seeking Friend
If you have no luck?
Come see Miss Suzie at
314/5 Villa Phan Thanh
Gian St. Saigon. This place
you can meet beautiful
charming high class girls
they want to make acquain-
tances, with foreigners, I
thing (sic) you'll be glad
you come.

PTT 92785
(from 0800-to-1900 daily)

Was it a coincidence that the addresses were so close to each other? "PTT" was the acronym for the French communications system known as *"Postes, Télégraphes et Téléphones."*

In the same paper, one could find one's horoscope ("Your Lucky Star"), Ann Landers' column, sports, the stock market, comics, and ads for hotels, night clubs and restaurants.

French is still spoken by the older bourgeois class and by many students at the *Alliance Française*, and the *Cercle Sportif.*

The American military presence is, of course, overwhelming; but there is also the lesser-known civilian side such as The *Seventh Day Adventist Hospital* on Hai Ba Trung, the *Abraham Lincoln Library* at 8, Le Qui Don, and the *Vietnamese-American Association* on Mac Dinh Chi. The square around the Saigon Cathedral is named J. F. Kennedy Square.

There are, of course, countless Vietnamese restaurants where one can sample the popular food:

Cha Gio: These are small rolls, similar to Chinese egg-rolls. The contents are prepared by mixing crabmeat, pork, noodles and chopped vegetables together, rolling them in a thin rice-paper wrapping, and deep-frying the finished delicacy.

Chao Tom: This dish comprises individual sticks of sugarcane, around which has been rolled a spiced shrimp paste, and which is then grilled. The flavor is delicious and haunting.

Bo Bay Mon: Literally translated this means Seven Beef Dishes and this is just what it is. Each dish is prepared in a different manner, and while some have vegetables added to them, others have the beef diced, sliced, minced or made into a paté. Each one is eaten in a special manner and they all have their own special and traditional sauces. This is a favorite with Americans in Saigon.

Com Tay Cam: This is a special treat that consists of a basic rice dish cooked in a covered earthen pot, with a mixture of mushrooms, chicken and pork, sliced very fine. The whole dish is served with a ginger sauce and this is truly a Mandarin's delight to taste.

Pho: This is a soup in which are mixed an infinite variety of choice morsels, depending on the traditions of the cook. Basically, it resembles a consommé prepared with beef or chicken and noodles. The bouillon or broth is very carefully prepared, the main beef and noodle ingredients being added at the last minute. In this manner the particularly delicate and unusual flavor of the broth is kept separate from that of the meat and other added ingredients. The result is a delicious blend of flavors that is absolutely unique. Pho should not be confused with the many varieties of *soupe chinoise* that are prepared from various bases and are indeed similar to the Tonkinese Pho. These soups provide an excellent late night supper before the nightclub reveler returns home.

The principal military newspaper is *The Pacific Stars and Stripes,* described as "An authorized unofficial publication for the US Armed Forces of the Pacific Command," price, 10 cents.

Other, more tabloid papers include the *Overseas Weekly,* called by some because of its liberal articles and photos, "Oversexed Weekly," and the *Grunt Free Press.* "You Don't Need Grass When You Have Grunt Free Press," as the paper itself displayed on its front page.

There is even a bilingual English/French newspaper, *The Vietnam Observer/ L'Observateur du Vietnam,* founded in 1966, located at 235 Hai Ba Trung, Saigon.

The number of Chinese newspapers has been estimated at more than ten, and Vietnamese language papers perhaps as high as 20.

Time and *Newsweek* are available locally in their Asian editions printed on ultra thin paper.

The traffic in the streets of Saigon is chaotic. Along with military jeeps and trucks there are innumerable bicycles, cyclos, cars, and buses of every size and description. A cyclo (pronounced "see-clo"), formerly called pedicab, replaced the coolie-pulled rickshaws of years ago. They are three-wheeled pedal-operated trishaws, which operate within the limits of Saigon. According to a tourist brochure:

Cyclos are comfortable three-wheeled bicycles – basically pedal-propelled arm-chairs, ideal for a smooth ride along the city's shady boulevards. The driver sits high up behind the passenger so that he can see over the cambriolage, the foldable canvas supported by thin metal bars and struts that can be raised as a shield for the rain. Many drivers are grizzled old men in pith helmet, ragged undershirt, shower sandals, shorts and a conical hat. You will see them flash their gold teeth in a big smile, or not, depending on the day and the amount of your tip. Some have a tinkly bicycle bell that they can use to attract potential passengers, and even sometimes out of frustration in traffic, as a horn, but it is really quite ludicrous. On occasion, to help an overweight or ungainly passenger to alight, the driver will tip the cyclo forward to assist the passenger out the vehicle.

Cyclo drivers, nearly naked, scratch and sleep by day, as they do by night. Sometimes they awoke and chewed betel for a while, spitting from time to time, till their lips were stained purple, and their thoughts were soothed again by its aromatic freshness, their eyes, as their mandibles moved slowly, gaining a ruminative, melancholy calm. Riding in a cyclo you feel the rhythmic side-to-side stretching and bending of the metal struts and canvas in unison with the driver's pushing down on the pedals. This was much more evident when going up the slight hills such as the one on Tu Do past the Continental.

A faster if less romantic way to travel Saigon's streets can be seen in the so-called "cyclo-mais" ("see-clo-mys") which are three-wheeled motor-driven vehicles resembling a motorcycle pushing an armchair. Their two-stroke "put-put" engines emit vast quantities of dense, blue smoke and make a loud sputtering sound unique to Saigon. A journey in a cyclo or cyclo-mai, not to mention a taxi, can be an adventure.

That evening when I returned to my room, there was a note from the villa manager:

TO: Villa Residents

The dining room and kitchens will be secured at 20:00 and no chow will be left out overnight. Due to pest problems residents are requested to not leave food items of any kind in Dining Room or TV Room area. No food will be served in rooms.

The "pests" referred to were the large rats that bred so easily among the piles of garbage in the streets. Local children played on them looking for something thrown away by the rich Americans.

At noon I would walk the long corridors of MACV to have lunch at the snack bar. Usually it was a sad-looking pot roast, lima beans, rice, milk, or just a grilled cheese sandwich. It was, as the name implies, just a small cafeteria where one took a tray and selected from the day's fare of basic typical American food. All the workers in the snack bar were Vietnamese, most of them women, though far different of course from the highly made-up and often beautiful women one saw in downtown Saigon.

At my desk there were always official memos to read. They would be passed around to everyone from carrel to carrel with the "cc" distribution list attached.

I had put up a large map of Vietnam on the wall of my small cubicle. The others came over to have a look. I was starting to settle in.

The *San Francisco Chronicle* reported that there are estimated to be about 200 to 300 VC sabotage experts in Saigon. The security situation did not look good.

The American Forces Vietnam Network (AFVN) with its motto "Serving the American fighting man twenty four hours a day from the Delta to the DMZ (Demilitarized Zone)" had some interesting "commercials," actually advice for GIs:

The going price for Saigon tea is 200P. One hundred of them will pay for that camera when you go on R&R.

I finally made a point of sending one of the maids to buy two new tires for my bike. This was the bike Roger had lent me and that he said I could now keep after I had fully repaired it. I paid only 725P altogether ($5.00 at the legal rate), including brake cable and rear reflector. I will try riding the bike to work every day if it is not too much of a pain. With a bike it's easy to squeeze around traffic and you can even pick it up and carry it if need be. I can ride on the little dirt paths that serve as sidewalks.

Back at the villa there was another note posted:

A guard has been hired to protect the villa area. His orders are to check in and out all non-resident visitors to the villa and to secure the villa gates after curfew.
Signed, The Manager.

The maids would also write notes regarding laundry procedures or meals:

Dear Sirs,
Would you please put your dirty clothes outside the door
before going to bed.
Thank you very much.
Hue

The security paranoia extended to one's private life as well. One morning, as I was just leaving my room to catch the van for MACV, Hue #1 had gathered up all my dirty clothes in her arms and was making off with them to the washing trough. I worried that some important note might be in one of my pockets and said, "Wait a minute, I have to look through the pockets." The sense of mistrust was heavily felt. One could not be sure that the Vietnamese who served you dinner would not slit your throat at night.

One evening at the villa, as we had just finished eating dinner, a large rat scampered under the table into the kitchen. The Vietnamese kids fearlessly went into the kitchen in their sandals and looked under the refrigerator. I rattled a mop under the fridge and when the rat came out I banged it on the head with the mop handle. "Wait," said someone, "I want to get my camera. I want to get a picture of this." I said, "Hurry up – run!" He did, and brought down his Polaroid camera as we all stood over the dead rat. The next day I put the photo over my desk at MACV with the caption "A Successful Combined Vietnamese-American Operation."

In the evening I tried to take a shower but there was no water again. Two weeks ago there was no electricity and, maybe today was a first for me – breakfast by candlelight. One of the villa residents had had enough of it and took a bath in the outdoor patio, took all his clothes off while the maids watched.

I studied the operations of the VCI and Phoenix as my trip to the Field was coming up soon.

From military and civilian documents, including RAND Corporation reports, I learned that the infrastructure, which was likened to the

Mafia, was composed of many organizations and committees, each with responsibility for specific functions.

These organizations were established hierarchically from hamlet to village, district, province, region, and finally at the level of various national headquarters.

At the apex of this structure stood the supreme headquarters: Central Office of South Vietnam. COSVN was the top command post for all communist activities in South Vietnam. It was responsible for both control of political affairs and direction of Viet Cong military activities.

COSVN itself reported directly to officials of the Vietnam Workers' Party in Hanoi. The key leaders of COSVN were members of the Central Executive Committee or Politburo of the Northern Party.

The physical location of COSVN headquarters was changed from time to time for security reasons. It was located in "War Zone D" northeast of Saigon in the early 1960's, and then moved to Tay Ninh province near the Cambodian border. The headquarters and the trails leading to it were camouflaged, according to a former cadre, and the top COSVN leaders had separate houses with underground shelters and escape tunnels.

With COSVN's efforts to conceal the North Vietnamese representation, its attempts to maintain secrecy for security reasons and its penchant for the use of code names, the identification of individual leaders was difficult. However, from captured documents and interrogation reports, a partial roster of the leadership could be constructed.

Cover designations and cover names were used extensively throughout the VC Infrastructure to conceal identities of both organizations and persons. Often one agency or one man had several designations. For example, Nguyen Chi Thanh was known as Sau Ri, Sau Di, Anh Sau, and Truong Son. In some cases the cover name for an individual in a high position would remain constant, even when the person in the position was changed. A famous instance of name changing was Ho Chi Minh, who was also known as Nguyen Ai Quoc, and by several other aliases.

Vietnamese were often referred to familiarly by the term "anh" (brother) and the number of the child in his family. The first child was numbered "one" in North Vietnam, but in the South the first born was numbered "two." This family name may be abbreviated with the letter "a" followed by a numeral, as "a7" for Anh Bay, "Brother Seven."

As the Party cadres gained power in the villages they began to regulate all aspects of each resident's life. Movement to and from areas controlled by the GVN (the legitimate Government of Viet Nam) was strictly monitored. Heavy taxes were levied and villagers were forced to house and feed VC troops as they moved through the area. There was a constant barrage of propaganda vilifying "the American imperialists and their Saigon puppet government."

Warning signals employed by villagers to alert Party cadres of impending GVN operations included: a woman calling her child in a special way, a woman wearing a special outfit, banging on pans in a prearranged manner, and beating on hand rattles or wooden fish.

In strong VC areas the village cadres lived in their own houses during the daytime, but changed sleeping places every night. Each of these houses had a secret cache in the floor, yard or orchard where they could hide when necessary.

In weak or contested VC areas, cadres could be expected to carry on their functions only at night and seldom for more than one hour in any given place.

Meetings involving high level cadres were held in the remotest hamlet of a strong VC village closest to a retreat base area. The hamlet and surrounding area would be riddled with underground caches. Normally a platoon or more of guerrillas formed a protective ring around the hamlet during the meeting to engage GVN forces long enough for the cadres to escape. A common warning signal was two shots when GVN forces were approaching in the distance.

In some hamlets, residents were forced to memorize precise responses to GVN search teams. For example:

Question: "Tell us which families hide the VC cadres so you won't be implicated."

Memorized Answer: "There are only Vietnamese living and earning their living here. The VC never come here."

Important cadres (Province or District level) were likely to travel with personal bodyguards and carry a concealed pistol.

Cadres often arose as early as 0430 hours to cook breakfast before smoke could be spotted. They remained concealed until after 1000 hours, since sweep operations normally occurred at dawn, if they occurred that day. Because the cities were controlled by the GVN, the VC cadre must live there legally and the individual cadre is permitted to know only his own immediate cell members. Meetings would often be held in a snack bar, soup shop, hospital or other crowded public place during the rush hours to avoid arousing suspicion.

The VC compiled blacklists of government officials, military officers, police, intelligence agents, and pacification cadres. The VC relied on an extensive network of secret agents and local informants, including even taxi and cyclo drivers whose mission was to determine the addresses of Vietnamese or Americans from the various military headquarters, and HQ MACV in particular.

The classification scheme used by the VC for individuals in their dossiers was very similar to our own. Category A individuals were prime candidates for elimination, with Category B second, and Category C considered marginal.

Assassinations and abductions in GVN-controlled hamlets were performed by the highly professional Armed Reconnaissance Units, or three-man "suicide cells." The individuals to be targeted, selected from the blacklists, were first reconnoitered thoroughly before being hit. Particulars including where and when he ate and slept, his route to and from work and any habits he might have such as prostitution, alcohol, or drugs. A blacklisted person was often killed at his own house or while on his way home from his office, when he was riding a bicycle or driving a car. They can lure him into a love trap or kill him during a party.

There was the Sapper Cell. "Sapper" is a military term originally denoting an engineer who is trained in demolition work. The term as applied to communist activities in South Vietnam was inaccurate, but, like the term Viet Cong, was in widespread use. The term meant a cell whose members used explosives in attacks on non-military targets.

Sapper cells operated chiefly in the urban areas. The majority were northerners. They worked with explosives and its members were expected to be able to handle TNT, dynamite, C-4 or plastique, the primary explosives used in Vietnam. The chief targets of the sapper cell were government buildings, American installations, communication and transportation centers, port and storage facilities, as well as vehicles, key enemy personnel, etc. One common method of the terrorist was the use of the bicycle or motorcycle with its hollow tubular frame packed with plastique and the timing device fixed under the saddle. The sapper rode into the area, leaned his machine against the building to be destroyed, set the fuse and walked off.

Tomorrow I would start my Field trip to the provinces and carry out my assignment on the Phoenix program for Ambassador Colby, a difficult task in the world of intelligence and counterterrorism. I grew more and more uneasy about this.

CHAPTER 3

Early in the morning our Vietnamese driver Bien picked me up in the Toyota. Our first destination was, as Colby had instructed me, Vung Tau, on the South China Sea. Vung Tau is a beach resort, a famous in-country R&R destination, and a center of training for Phoenix operatives and the RD Cadre, the Revolutionary Development Cadre. It is known as *Cap Saint-Jacques* to the French. It's about 40 miles southeast of Saigon as the helicopter flies, but by road it is more like 75 miles, since it is necessary to take the more secure route north on the Bien Hoa Highway, then east and south. After the wide Bien Hoa Highway the road narrows to one lane each way and axle-breaking potholes lurk around every turn.

Most of the traffic was going in our direction. Many Honda drivers and passengers are outfitted with handkerchiefs over their faces against the clouds of exhaust and dust spewed up by military trucks.

As we crossed the Saigon River we could see the freighters being offloaded, barges moving slowly along, and the rusty, corrugated metal shacks huddled along the river bank between the greenish brown water and thick banana trees. The long bridge we were crossing was shored up by large steel braces as it had been recently blown up by the VC. They had driven a car loaded with explosives to the middle of it, set them off and jumped into the river.

Once across the bridge, which like all key targets had sandbagged and barbed wire guard posts at each of its four corners, we drove through typical hamlets with thatched, grey-brown huts surrounded by huge banana palms.

It was hot and humid. When our truck slowed down or stopped there was no more cooling breeze and sweat ran down into our eyes.

Passing through the small village of Thu Duc, we were forced to stop behind a long line of army trucks and every other kind of vehicle imaginable. Local women, taking advantage, walked from car to truck to motorbike peddling bananas, mangoes, and ice cream. A beggar stopped and looked pleadingly into our Toyota. He appeared to be almost blind. I took some coins out of my pocket and put them in his hand.

The traffic jam finally cleared up and we got underway again. With every pothole, the truck bounced up and down, doors and teeth rattling.

A half hour from our destination we ran into another traffic jam inside a small hamlet. All the locals were out enjoying the spectacle. Hondas and Lambrettas were buzzing and revving their engines like a swarm of angry bees. Unbelievably, there was an old Desoto bus, packed to overflowing with dark-skinned, little Vietnamese, all straining to look out the windows, many rows of white teeth showing in wide grins. Also clogging the narrow road were deuce and a halfs carrying armed troops.

All traffic was frozen because vehicles on both sides of the road had attempted to pass and, if they had continued would have run into each other. So there were two lanes of traffic going south and two lanes going north on a two-lane road.

There were troops of all nationalities, American, Vietnamese, Australian, Korean, and Thai. Two sweating MPs were talking to a group of GIs. I asked them what the trouble was. "There's an Aussie tank turned over on the side of the road." Sure enough, we could see far ahead a big crane sticking up in the air, apparently what is called a 'Tank Recovery Vehicle.' We were told by an MP who had seen our cameras that there was an Aussie tank overturned up ahead and not to take pictures of it, as it was a "special" tank; otherwise, our cameras would be confiscated. We finally got going and crept along for a few hundred feet, passing by the tank which was almost on its side, deeply sunk into the soft shoulder. There were other huge tanks in front and behind it but we thought it best not to take pictures.

After crossing a couple more rickety bridges, we pulled into Vung Tau. From our vantage point on a hill we could see the curving, rocky sea coast. It was sparsely inhabited. We first went to see the RD Cadre. The training facility was in a corrugated metal compound with classrooms and barracks, a chow hall, lecture rooms and of course rifle ranges. There were some American instructors and the chief administrator was also an American. The cadre themselves wear black pajamas, collar-less shirt, and black 'ranger' hat.

Quoting from the RD Cadre Training Manual:

Springing from the people, the RD cadre have been at work in the countryside of Vietnam since 1965 in response to the political chaos existing since the overthrow of President Diem in 1963.

Some day when 'the rains are right and the wind is good,' the people will rise up from their obscurity to rid themselves of the shame of backwardness and insecurity.

The RD cadres are trained to be capable of fighting the communists and carrying out construction and development tasks in place of the government agencies which cannot work in the hamlets due to lack of security.

Each thirty-man RD cadre group is placed under the operational control and command of a village chief.

After the inspection and lectures at the RD Cadre Center, I wanted to take a look at the famous Vung Tau beach. The first long stretch of beach we saw, near the main part of town, looked a bit oily so we proceeded up a hill and around the shoreline to another section.

As Vung Tau is an in-country R&R center, Americans are a common sight, though even here vastly outnumbered by Vietnamese. We stopped at a bistro overlooking the sea. There was a large sign out front in French, *Hotel & Restaurant Plage au Vent*. Another place we'd seen on the way in was called *Auberge des Roches Noires*. Their ad as it appeared in the newspapers:

Où Trouver
Calme et Détente?
("Where to find calm and relaxation?")
Week-end a l'Auberge des Roches Noires
Bai Dua Vung Tau
Spécialité maison: sa bouillabaisse

We sat at a table with a view of the sea and ordered some beers which, to our pleasant surprise, were actually cold. A rusty Czech freighter had run aground several years ago while trying to smuggle arms to the VC and it sat high and dry on the beach. Its prow was a good sixty feet above the hard, flat, sandy beach. Some Vietnamese kids were climbing up its huge, rusting anchor chain. It looked like a long way up. After the beers, we walked down the many flights of stairs to the beach. There was a mix of Vietnamese families and American GIs, some with girlfriends, lounging on the beach.

Returning to Saigon before dark was imperative as the roads were not secure at night. The Aussie tank was still in the ditch and again a traffic jam held us up. We got out and talked to some rifle-carrying Aussie soldiers from the tank itself who were standing around the scene. When told that the American MP had said the tank was "special," they laughed and said, "Bullshit! Special cuz it's stuck."

Darkness was creeping in and we were getting nervous and kept checking our watches to see how much time there was left before dark. When the traffic snarl finally cleared up and we were able to get going again, we drove at top speed, passing everything in our way.

As we rolled into Saigon, the sun had set and the city was preparing for night.

Next day I got ready for the big trip to the Field where the real work for Colby would begin. I would be traveling again by Toyota Land Cruiser, this time to the provinces of Long Khan and Phuoc Tuy in III Corps (later known as Military Region III), an area that comprised eleven provinces between the Central Highlands and the Mekong River Delta.

My travel orders, issued by Headquarters MACV were, according to standard practice, written in military short-hand or "telegramese."

HEADQUARTERS
UNITED STATES MILITARY ASSISTANCE COMMAND,
VIETNAM
APO San Francisco 96222
MACAG

Frank Wadleigh

> LETTER ORDERS
> NUMBER 10-1314
> SUBJECT: Blanket Travel Orders

> *TC 204. Indiv directed to pro fr dy sta indic at intervals, with itin, and
> dest wi RVN presb by aprop auth. No exp to the Govt WB incurred by reason
> of TDY and tvl. RPSCTDY.*
>> *Purpose: Collection and analysis of CORDS data*
>> *Sp instr: 66 lbs acmp air bag auth. Indiv auth to carry wpn.*

I got a chuckle out of the phrase, "No expense to the government will
be incurred." Well, who IS going to pay for it? I thought. Are they going
to send me a bill?

In preparation for the trip, I reviewed the characterizations of A, B,
C, D, and E categorized hamlets and examined the Terrorist Incident
Reporting System (TIRS) overlays of maps of Long Khanh and Phuoc Tuy
provinces to see where most acts of terrorism had occurred. As a security
measure, the Army compound in Xuan Loc had phoned HQ MACV to
find out my ETA.

In the morning we left Saigon and, after some difficulty getting
through a traffic-congested Phan Thanh Gian, crossed the bridge from
Dakao out to Highway 1 and arrived in Xuan Loc, capital of Long Khanh
Province, about 12:15, having covered the 70 kilometers fairly easily.

On arrival at the U. S. Army compound we were met by the Province
Senior Advisor (PSA) of Long Khanh Province, a lieutenant colonel.

After stowing our gear, the PSA drove me by jeep to the Kiem Tan
District compound.

Kiem Tan District consisted of 5 villages and 25 hamlets. The DSA
(District Senior Adviser) was a captain who, though only a month in
country, seemed very knowledgeable. The first order of business being the
HES, I asked him some standard questions including how long it took for
the advisers to fill out the HES questionnaires. He said about 30 hours
a month. He then presented his summary of the security situation in the
district:

"In this district there is a large catholic majority; in fact, the priests
have more authority than the hamlet chiefs.

42

"Militarily, the VC are targeting the People's Self Defense Force (PSDF). Two recent assassinations of members occurred in Le Loi hamlet on Route 20 about three kilometers north of Route 1. Notes were pinned to bodies giving the reason that victims had passed information to US/GVN. Since the latter had received no significant intelligence information, this led to speculations that the victim had unsuspectingly passed information on to a VC agent.

"Another problem is poor leadership of the PF."

The PF, or Popular Force, was a form of local militia responsible for providing security at the village level. There was also the RF, or Regional Force, responsible for security at the district level. They were jointly designated as 'RF/PF.'

"They conduct their ambushes by sitting 30 meters or so outside of the hamlet and in more or less the same spot every night so it's no problem for a VC sympathizer to direct them through this so-called ambush."

The Captain also said it was difficult to schedule B-52 strikes on an important north-south VC supply route east of Route 20 as sometimes only three to four hours advance notice was given, not enough time to get our troops out.

Curfew here was 1900 along highways. Anything out after then, lights on or not, was fair game for friend or foe.

Excerpts from the PSA's official security summary:

A thorough re-evaluation of the HES in every hamlet was made by the District Senior Advisors, resulting in five hamlets being downgraded from a B security status to C.

The province had 79.7% of the population in AB, meaning classification A or B.

Although the goal for eliminating VCI was met, the Phung Hoang Program is not at a satisfactory level yet. Twenty (20) VCI were neutralized and 44 sentenced. During the entire year 239 VCI were neutralized.

Several PSDF (People's Self Defense Force) members and hamlet officials were specifically targeted and executed by the Viet Cong.

Terrorist and assassination incidents also increased with 5 personnel assassinated. All of these assassinations were against hamlet officials or PSDF members, pointing up the enemy's efforts to disrupt the GVN pacification program.

The PSA told me that we would have to leave the DSA Compound by 1630 as convoys came down about this time from Dinh Quan. We took his advice and arrived back in Xuan Loc in time for dinner at 1830.

The dining area in the CORDS compound occupied the left part of the main room. At the head of the long dining table was the PSA with the DPSA (Deputy PSA) at the other end. Seated along the sides of the table were the National Police Adviser, the RF/PF adviser, a civilian agricultural adviser, another major, and two other civilians. Leading off from this large central dining room were library room, TV room, kitchen, and bedrooms.

The evening meal consisted of soup, fried chicken, string beans, and French fries. Water was served instead of the usual iced tea. Dinner time provided an opportunity for everyone to get together to review the happenings of the day.

I asked the colonel about the overall security situation.

"You really ought to talk to the Catholic priest here," he said. "He knows what's going on with the people and has been here for a long time. We call him the almighty priest of the 'Vatican,' that is, the head priest of Xuan Loc. He doesn't speak any English though, only Vietnamese and French."

"My French isn't too bad," I said, understating the French I had learned not only at university but as a student in Paris. "OK, I'll have a meeting set up for you tomorrow morning."

"Fine, thanks," I said.

After dinner, we walked across the street to the recreation area which consisted of a big screen outdoor movie theater and a bar area covered by a corrugated tin roof. I bought a beer and wandered over to the "dance floor" where young Vietnamese girls in mini-skirts were dancing with GIs. Others were sitting at tables, laughing and drinking beer. The jukebox was playing the perennial GI favorites: *Sugar, Sugar,* and *We Gotta Get Out of This Place.*

We stayed the night in the Xuan Loc CORDS compound. Inside my sleeping quarters, a sign on the door informed guests:

DEAR VISITORS:
THE CHARGE FOR THIS ROOM IS 50 PIASTERS PER
NIGHT FOR MAID SERVICE – LAUNDRY INCLUDED.
ALL MEALS ARE $1.00 US OR 118 PIASTRE (sic) EACH
PLEASE PAY THE CASHIER IN CHARGE
THE GREATER XUAN LOC MAFIA

Accommodations in the compound were a lot better than I had expected: twin beds, private bathroom with shower, and even a small refrigerator. There was no air conditioning but the ceiling fan was adequate. The floor was tiled as usual and the seven foot high ceiling had sound-absorbent board. The walls were covered with thin wood paneling. The letters "USAID" were stenciled on the bed frames.

From my bed that night I could hear noises of some animal gnawing on leftovers in the kitchen. Hope it's just a dog or a cat, I mused.

The next day I was up at 0600 and, before the chopper ride up north to Dinh Quan, we listened to Nixon's speech on the transistor radio. He cited the British guerilla war expert Sir Robert Thompson's optimism after his visit to Vietnam.

At breakfast the DPSA notified me that the chopper will be ready to pick me up at 0815.

A colonel suddenly burst in the door.

"Where's Smith?"

One of the officers says, "He's taking someone on a tour today and won't be back till late."

"*I'm* the one he's supposed to be taking," he thundered, to which general laughter.

Smith was the National Police advisor. When he finally arrived, he reported that the Police compound, about one and a half kilometers from here, had been mortared the previous night. They had found two tailfins of B40 rocket propelled grenades. Some damage was incurred but no casualties. At dinner later that day, we learned that seven policemen had been jailed for negligence on account of the incident. The policemen had not fired back because they claimed they were in direct line with a PF ambush.

At 0800 I went in the DPSA's jeep out to the heliport. I carried, in addition to a carbine, an empty briefcase to bring back some of the hand-made mahogany bowls and candlestick holders I had heard about. They were made by an opium-smoking old man out in the boonies. He operated a foot-powered lathe to craft the mahogany into beautiful creations.

When I climbed aboard the Huey chopper, the pilot and copilot were already aboard. A Vietnamese civilian sat in front of me in one of the two canvas-covered metal seats. As everyone scrambled to buckle their seat belts, the noise of the motor and blades was so deafening that even shouting could not be heard. The Vietnamese civilian scribbled on a scrap of paper, "I am the Deputy District Chief of Dinh Quan District, and you?" He handed me the note and I quickly wrote underneath, "MACV Saigon, HES program," and passed it back. He read it, looked back over his shoulder at me and we exchanged smiles and nods of introduction.

Port and starboard machine gunners, each wearing a special helmet with headphones and microphone, climbed aboard and, as the blades whirled faster and faster, the Huey lifted off, a short takeoff down the asphalt runway, not a vertical liftoff but rising gradually like a small plane.

It was misty that morning and everything was soaking wet from the previous night's rain shower so it was still not really bright. Once above the village we climbed higher, barely clearing the rubber trees, and then a bit higher still we popped out of the mist into a clear blue sky. There were vast plantations of rubber trees, bent from the strong winds that always came from the same direction, the whole resembling from the air the curving bristles on an old broom.

The pilot followed the bends and curves in Route 20, the main "highway." As the road jogged sharply to the right and up a hill, the chopper followed, banking at almost 60 degrees so that looking out one side all you could see was the sky, and out the other straight down was the ground. The port gunner had a camera and snapped a few photos as we passed over small hamlets, some fairly prosperous with cement-block houses, others poor, with shacks made of boards and corrugated tin roofs. In bigger hamlets, clustered into compact villages stretching along the highway, church spires were visible.

I noticed that the pilot and copilot/navigator were looking at a map as we passed over a US Army engineer compound set up for improvement of Route 20 to make it a MACV "Standard Road." After circling twice around the compound filled with construction supplies and equipment, someone on the ground below stepped out of a jeep and waved us in.

We descended and settled down on a steel pad in a cloud of whirling dust. We got off the chopper and were picked up in a jeep driven by a captain from the District Adviser's compound on the other side of the road. The compound was a one-story, heavy wood construction with corrugated metal roofing, a relatively substantial building.

For almost the entire morning we sat at the dining table for our discussions. Aside from a small radio room to the side, everything, dining area as well as the kitchen, was in the one room. There was a TV set in the corner, a couch with coffee table on which were lying some old Playboy magazines. A couple of Vietnamese lacquer paintings adorned the walls.

Out in back were the lavatories. The guys told the story that to blow out a hole for the urinal, they had accidentally used a 40-pound shape charge and the entire "can" was blown far up and away down the road; windows were blown out, refrigerators blasted open, the whole place covered with dust. The officers were roaring with laughter while telling this story.

This part of Route 20 was well paved with asphalt but not really wide, just adequate for two vehicles. This was the main highway between Dalat and Saigon, and buses of all shapes and sizes rumbled by, most of which were dilapidated, dusty and packed with travel-weary Vietnamese wearing the usual straw conical hats to shelter them from the sun.

Traffic was much heavier in the direction of Saigon. There were buses with luggage racks on the roof piled high with furniture, chairs, tables, everything strapped down, entire families on the move. Large, black Citroëns with "Saigon-Dalat" written in large letters above their windshields had been conscripted as buses on this route, and were packed with refugees. There were also Honda motorcycles towing three-wheeled carts carrying up to five Vietnamese. Many of the passengers were old women clutching at parcels and market produce.

The village of Dinh Quan was comprised of four hamlets: Tin Nghia, the biggest one, Trung Hieu, Trung Van Phu, and a montagnard hamlet to the south.

The compound of the District Senior Adviser of Dinh Quan District was located about 60 yards south of the helipad on the opposite side of route 20. It was therefore, on the west side of the highway and amid several large rock formations. These large boulders were made of granite and it was contested whether their origin was volcanic or glacier. If they existed only in the vicinity of Dinh Quan village itself that would contradict the glacier theory of formation. The volcanic theory, on the other hand, seemed more reasonable. Most of the rock formations consisted of two, three, or even four huge boulders one on top of the other, very precisely and well-fitted, rising anywhere from 30 to 70 feet. They looked like piles of huge granite dice.

On the other side of the RF compound was another rock formation, reaching perhaps as high as 70 feet, on top of which was a circular sandbagged bunker area and other fortifications. This belonged to the PF platoon. Between the rock formations were scattered mines, old, unmarked ones laid by the French and also new ones laid by the Vietnamese. However, access between rocks was prevented by fences and barbed wire.

At noon the "mamasan" (as the GIs called her) made us lunch of sliced ham, tomato salad, and beans.

The DSA of Dinh Quan had been in this post for seven months of this, his second tour of Vietnam. He was sitting at the big dining table looking over some of the many reports he had to read and sign.

In a couple of minutes he put down his work and jumped up to greet us, then pulled out a map and a sheaf of HES reports.

He indicated that in the HES set of village questions, the requirement that in answering a question on security, the term "village" must include the total geographical area. This made it impossible to report accurately on the security situation, since the population lived almost exclusively in a very small area along the main highway. In the village of Dinh Quan, for example, much of the village area included portions of "War Zone D." If this area (where part of the NVA 5th Division was located) must be included in a security question, the result would not show the true security situation. He suggested adding a separate village question to reflect conditions in both inhabited and uninhabited areas.

He gave a summary of the situation in Dinh Quan:

"There are two Mobile Advisory Teams, or MAT Teams, as they are redundantly called. One is permanently stationed at the bridge, along with an RF company, the other temporarily in the north. The bridge was blown up in June, 1968.

"The religious makeup in Dinh Quan District is 40% catholic and 60% Buddhist. Truck farming is the primary source of income ever since logging had cleared both sides of the highway.

"Lumber, especially mahogany, is second in the economy. The loggers are government licensed and must pay taxes to both the GVN and the VC. Since the loggers must work in the jungles where the VC are hiding, they must pay taxes to the VC.

"The principal rice-growing area is located in the southeast portion of Dinh Quan District; the district is now nearly self-sufficient in this essential food.

"Loi Thanh is an all Chinese hamlet with a low security rating. There were two assassinations on the 20th of November. There is much profiteering but one shopkeeper refused to sell to the VC.

"The VC stay, for the most part, in the jungle, except for forays into the hamlets at night. A flagrant exception is Loi Tan where the VC pose as farmers during the day, making certain they get their share of food. The Chinese have a neutral attitude toward GVN and VC, their primary concern being to make money as shopkeepers. They sell to both sides. Recently, however, a Chinese shopkeeper was assassinated by the VC for having taken payment for rice but failing to deliver. On the other hand, a Chinese also from Loi Tan was caught about three weeks ago by the National Police with a load of supplies for the VC.

"Farmers are often forced to leave packets of food at the edges of fields for the VC to pick up at night. They may even have small plots of land apart from the main fields on which they grow food for the VC. A possible solution to this problem is to have the PF stationed at strategic points around the fields so that when pressured by VC to give food the farmer can look up and see the PF and have someone to back him up so he can safely refuse to cooperate."

The evening after returning from Dinh Quan, I was having a beer with the PSA in his mobile trailer. There was a knock on the door. It was a major.

"The RF compound in Binh Hoa village has taken 60 mortar rounds and a lieutenant is in there and it's too late to get him out."

"He'll just have to remain in the bunker overnight. Keep me informed," said the colonel, and the major left.

The next morning I visited with the village priest, Père (Father) Chum, at the local cathedral. He was an older man and cheerfully greeted me in French. I explained that I was from HQ in Saigon and wanted to know the security situation in Xuan Loc. We spoke outdoors in the heat of the day. In fluent, Vietnamese-accented French, he told me that of the total village population of 30,000, approximately 12,000 are Catholic. He said he had come here from North Vietnam in the late 1950's. The North Vietnamese had made it very difficult for him to leave. Now, however, it's impossible to get out of North Vietnam.

"The Michelin rubber plantation is still run by the French," he said.

"Do they pay VC taxes?" I inquired.

"Yes, but the money actually changes hands in Paris."

"How strong is the VC here?"

"A major VC concentration is located between Xuan Loc village and Route 20. During Tet '68 they circled south of the village, then east and north to harass the 18th ARVN Division," he said, making a wide sweeping gesture with his arm in that general direction. "An RF company is now assigned to patrol this area."

"We, the Catholic Church, are building a new school for the village. It will be completed next year. The village needs a central market place located outside of the village center. This is because of security problems resulting from overcrowded conditions. The VC go into the market place and extort food from the merchants."

When I asked him about the feelings of the locals, he said, "The majority of the people are in favor of the government and President Thieu but Vietnamese are very jealous of their independence."

I thanked him for the opportunity to ask questions.

We left Xuan Loc at 1215 the next day after first tanking up at the local Shell station and taking a few pictures of the town. We then drove out to have a look at the famous Michelin rubber plantation. Due to the fact that the road from Xuan Loc to Phuoc Le was not secure, we took Route 1 to

Long Binh, stopping at the O Club (Officers' Club) for lunch. At 1430 we left Bien Hoa, traveling down Route 15, and arrived 1550 in Phuoc Le.

Phuoc Le, the capital of Phuoc Tuy Province, was also known as Ba Ria for one of the early settlers of the area, a woman by the name of Tia Ria.

After driving around town looking for a building flying the American flag, indicating a military post, we found instead an official-looking building with a Vietnamese flag and went in to inquire. A US Army lieutenant was there and volunteered to take me to the CORDS office where I met the PSA who gave me, with the aid of a wall map, a quick rundown on the situation in Phuoc Tuy Province.

The PSA said, "The message we received was that you had left Xuan Loc and were headed south on Route 2. We were concerned. A Vietnamese truck was mined on Route 2. This road is practically suicide south of Blackhorse. There are no ARVN troops in the province and no American troops either."

The lieutenant said he would try to get a chopper to take me up to see Duc Thanh.

We unloaded the Toyota, put our gear in our respective rooms, and drove out to find the DSA. On the way, a jeep driven by a US Army major passed us going in the opposite direction at breakneck speed. I guessed that this was the DSA. When we arrived at the compound this was confirmed.

The DSA had left quickly, it was explained, because the PF unit had just killed a VC; not just any VC, but the VCI Party Secretary. They had seen him crossing a field and had zapped him. They said the wife or mother would probably come out to claim the body so they would leave it lying there as bait, knowing that it wouldn't be long before one of them would be out and then they could zap her too.

I went to see the DSA and when I found him I asked if this man had been targeted as a VCI prior to his being killed, and what was his classification. And why was it necessary to kill his wife or mother?

"This is part of the Phoenix program," said the DSA. "It's the Provincial Reconnaissance Units, or PRUs. We have nothing to do with this."

I asked him, "Of the 2,000 or so that were found dead on the battlefield, how many had dossiers on file identifying them as class A or class B VCI?"

"This information is at the Province Interrogation Center, or PIC," he said.

I said, "Can you take me to the PIC?"

"I've never been there."

"Why is this?"

"Because it is operated by the CIA."

I said, "You must be kidding."

"I only know that from rumor. No one has proven that to me as a fact, but I have been told not to go near the Province Interrogation Center, because that is not within the responsibility of CORDS or the military advisers. That is a CIA operation."

I insisted, under the aegis of my assignment from Ambassador Colby, that I be shown the PIC. The DSA finally consented and had me driven there in a jeep.

At the PIC I was met by two American civilians. After asking them and showing my credentials, they finally admitted that they were working for the CIA.

The PIC in Phuoc Tuy province was constructed inside an abandoned school. False walls had been built so as to leave the observer with the impression that the school building was empty and abandoned. Along a central corridor were 24 cells, each five by seven feet with only a small 12-inch slit at the top to admit air. On the other side of the corridor were slightly larger interrogation cells. A ten foot wall surrounded the building, with a steel gate that hid the view from outside.

Inside the PIC a wanted poster with the Phoenix bird at the top was pinned to the wall. It gave the photo and name of the VC cadre that the Phung Hoang was looking for, listed his alias(es), mother's name, father's name, and position in the VCI. The poster offered a reward and, crucially, anonymity for the individual notifying the police.

What alarmed me and disturbed me about the CIA operating the Province Interrogation Centers was that this was the most sensitive part of the entire Phoenix program. This was where the prisoner was taken in order to question him and get a confession. It was also disturbing that there was a necessity for a cover for the CIA in the operation of the PIC.

Once a detainee had gone through a process of interrogation for up to 45 days at the PIC he would go before the Province Security Committee (PSC). The PSC did not have the function of finding guilt or innocence; they only had the function of establishing the length of the sentence.

Each village had a Village Intelligence Operations Coordination Center (VIOCC) where information was collected and sent to the DIOCC, the District Intelligence Operations Coordination Center, where it was further processed and programmed into "dossiers," files on categories A or B suspects in the Phoenix program.

If an individual was in the top level Viet Cong Infrastructure, according to the three intelligence sources in his dossier, he was listed as category A and was then "targeted."

An individual was called a "category B suspect" if there was in his dossier intelligence from three sources simply linking him with the VCI.

If he had no such references in his dossier, he was marked as category C. He may have expressed some disagreement with the South Vietnamese government in Saigon.

The PSC consisted of seven members, The Province Chief, the Chief of the Court of that province, a representative of the Province Council, the intelligence officer of the ARVN, the National Police Chief of the province, the Military Security service chief, and the Political Service chief of Internal Security of the province.

The PSC met once a week, on Friday, generally between 9 and 12 in the morning, during which time they averaged about 40 to 50 cases. The defendant was not permitted to be present. There was no defense attorney.

I was really disgusted and upset about what I had seen and heard regarding this Phoenix program and I wrote a rough draft of a memo I would circulate once I got back to Saigon.

CHAPTER 4

At Headquarters there was a new memo:

TO: AC of S (Assistant Chief of Staff), CORDS:

In conformance with COMUS' directive, please eliminate the word "blacklist" from Page 4. I suggest that an appropriate substitute for this word can be "VCI list."

More euphemisms. I thought the best first step in figuring out what to do about the killings that had happened while I was in the field would be to talk it over with my boss, Mike Brown, the one who had interviewed me in LA.

As usual in the morning I cycled to work and then from my desk walked across the hall to Mike's office.

"I'd like to make an appointment to see Mike, if I could," I said to the secretary.

"Sure, how about right after lunch?"

"Fine, thanks."

I thought it would be good to have written the Field Trip Report by the time I saw Mike. I wrote it up and gave it to Roger to type, and it was ready by noon. After a quick lunch in the cafeteria I strode down the long corridors of MACV, eventually reaching Mike's office.

Inside, I said, "Can I shut the door?"

"Sure, go ahead." Mike suddenly looked concerned.

"You know I just came back from my field trip."

"Yes of course. How did it go?"

"Oh it went fine, very interesting, but some pretty surprising things happened. I mean I found out some really, at least for me, shocking things."

"Such as?"

"The Vietnamese military shot a suspected VC in a field, then lay in wait for the wife or mother of the dead man to come out so they could zap her too."

"Well, you know women can also be VC."

"Not only that, but it seems the CIA is playing a key part, not just an advisory role, in certain vital parts of the Phoenix program."

"Oh?" Mike said casually.

"Yes, they actually run the PICs, the Provincial Interrogation Centers."

"No, that's not possible; the PICs are entirely run by the Vietnamese."

"Yes, that's what I thought, but when I asked the DSA in Phuoc Tuy if he had been to the PIC he said he had never been to the PIC because that is a CIA operation."

"Oh no. I don't think so," Mike said, shaking his head.

"I can't believe that the CIA is operating the PICs. That's the most sensitive part of the entire Phoenix program. This is where civilians are interrogated to get a confession. I really think we should pass this information on to someone who can do something about it. This Phoenix program seems very brutal to me; arresting, murdering civilians without a trial."

"Listen," Mike urged, "I think you've been given some wrong info here. Don't forget there is a war going on. I know sometimes it's hard to believe, being here in Saigon. It can be a dirty war. In every war there are these isolated incidents."

It seemed to me that I wasn't getting anywhere, so I just opted out, saying, "OK, I just wanted you to know about it."

"All right," said Mike, "and good work on the Field Trip Report."

That evening after work I cycled back to my room and decided that I needed a cold beer, and maybe more, to de-stress from recent happenings. I took a cold shower to cool off from the humid Saigon heat. You wanted to take a cold shower to cool off but the water never was really cold and when you got out of the shower you started to sweat right away as you struggled to put your clothes on. I then walked up the couple of blocks to Dakao. Along the way, on the corner of Mac Dinh Chi and Phan Thanh Gian, I passed several groups of Vietnamese soldiers armed with rifles.

When I walked into Flora's I sat at the bar and ordered the usual "Ba Muoi Ba," or "33" beer, and looked around at the scene of girls talking with their current partners. Ba Muoi Ba, or "Bamba," was said to contain 12 percent formaldehyde and was well known for giving those morning-after headaches, but it was cheap. I ended up taking home the girl we called "Greendress." She had a great figure. In Saigon it wasn't permitted for a Vietnamese girl and an American male to ride together in a car or taxi, so we went separately to my room, she by taxi, and me leading the way on my bicycle.

The next day I felt relieved in a sense, a new lease on life, although this one had been strictly for "medicinal purposes." She was one of those "I love you too much" types.

Lunch time at MACV I liked to escape from the artificial, air-conditioned Headquarters building where I was confined for so many hours a week. I would cross the road to Tan Son Nhut, one of the world's busiest airports. In the restaurant I always ordered a bowl of Chinese noodle soup consisting of thin noodles, pieces of chicken, ham, beef, and vegetables in a broth spiced with red peppers. Chopsticks can get up most of the noodles except the really long ones that had to be slurped into the mouth. A ceramic spoon was supplied for the broth. The soup cost a mere 100P.

At Tan Son Nhut there was an incredible mix of sleek, jet fighters and wide-bodied military transports. Most commercial airlines were represented: *China Airlines, Cathay Pacific, Air Vietnam, Royal Air Lao, Air France, Royal Air Cambodge,* as well as *Pan Am,* of course. Planes and helicopters of all vintages and sizes cluttered the tarmac.

Occasionally, one might spot a plane belonging to *Air America,* the "clandestine" airline that everyone knew was run by the CIA. It was on charter from a civilian airline facade called "The Pacific Corporation." Military passengers were met and assisted by representatives of their respective services while civilians were greeted by gracious hostesses dressed in the traditional ao dai. Most of the men were in uniform, American or

South Vietnamese. Many Vietnamese civilians seemed to have hardened faces and one felt an air of hostility, especially in the faces of the slight, bony-faced men. There were continuous streams of Vietnamese walking as though marching in step across the tarmac to their planes. The women carried their provisions and belongings in netted bags.

At other times I would escape to an area behind Headquarters. There was an incongruous rural-like hamlet that was incredibly in contrast to MACV Headquarters. It was as though a peaceful, idealized hamlet out in the boonies had been transplanted there. I liked to call it the "model hamlet." It was rural Vietnam in miniature. All this was just a hundred yards from the multimillion dollar high-tech computer complex and nerve center of the war. Here in the "countryside" I could take a deep breath and relax, just the tonic I needed against the stress of work. The smell of the dark earth, the peasants toiling and laughing; it was all so uncomplicated and real. It was good to hear the crow of the rooster.

From inside this peaceful hamlet the entire war seemed a distant, crazy, unnecessary exercise. On second thought, the war was really much worse than crazy.

The poet Tennyson had said it:

The Two Voices

I wonder'd, while I paced along:
The woods were fill'd so full with song,
There seemed to be no room for wrong ....

As often as possible I would try to get away and find a perspective here in this lovely rural setting.

What should I do about this Phoenix situation? I really had to talk with someone and who better than my good friend Earl. When I returned to the office I asked him if he wanted to go to our Chinese restaurant in Cholon, that I had something to talk over with him. He readily agreed. It would be good to see what Earl, an old timer here in Vietnam, would say about my experiences in the field. Cholon was always suspected to be a VC area. One gets a taxi, is driven out of Saigon along the Boulevard Tran Hung Dao and then suddenly you are in China.

That evening after work I met Earl and we took one of those taxis in Saigon, painted in distinctive light blue and cream, little old French Renaults resembling toy cars. They were usually run down inside, upholstery removed and, in some of them, the whole interior was painted red. Drivers were usually old men who drove shoeless. One anxiously watched the driver's barefoot toes curl over the tiny, squeaking brake pedal as he pushed it down frantically to the floor. Then at night, like the French, they raced around with dim amber parking lights, if any, which they blinked up at intersections. They thought nothing of driving the wrong way up a one-way street, especially at night when they said, "It's nighttime and nobody cares anymore."

Cholon, perhaps the largest Chinese city outside of China, was founded by Chinese immigrants in the 18th century. Cholon is noisier, more crowded, less orderly, and more Asian than Saigon. Its streets are narrower and the shops are more like those of a bazaar.

In the early days of the French, Cholon was infamous for gambling, prostitution, and opium. The government farmed out the gambling business to an underworld organization called the *Grand Monde* (Great World). It was the largest such establishment in the world and almost all the economic resources of Vietnam were under the control of the Chinese. There were constant wars fought between those who would control this racket, the Binh Xuyen, backed by the Emperor himself, the Vietminh, and even the police, each wanting a monopoly.

Everything was on sale, aphrodisiacs running the gamut from rhinoceros horn to tiger's liver. Nothing was immoral as there was no morality.

Running through Cholon is the *Arroyo Chinois* (Chinese arroyo), a colorful half river, half canal, its rotting junks hull to hull, forming a huge floating village where thousands of Chinese sampans bring unprocessed rice paddy from the interior of the country. Hundreds of thousands of people live in straw huts sunk in the mud in a tangle of sampans and barges. Whole families, packed into makeshift shelters on these boats, spread out into Saigon and Cholon during the day looking for work.

For Americans, the favorite Chinese restaurant in Cholon was *Dong Khanh*, an ornate palace of gourmet oriental cuisine where there was the magic and feeling of escape that could only be attained in Cholon. Dragons and Phoenixes adorned the walls and wrapped themselves around columns up to the high ceilings.

Earl and I were whisked to a small table in a corner. The large, round tables were filled with Vietnamese and Chinese families.

Earl also had a passion for the crazy and unorthodox things in life. In this we were on the same wavelength. He asked how the trip had gone, so it was easier for me to get to the point. As the waiter handed us the menu, I started to tell him.

"When I was in Phuoc Tuy they shot a suspected VCI guy in the field and let him lie there waiting for his wife or mother to come retrieve him. Then they zapped her as well."

"Jesus!" said Earl.

"I asked the DSA if the victim had been targeted as a VCI before being killed, what was his classification, and then why was it necessary to kill his wife or mother?

"He told me that it's the PRUs, the Provincial Reconnaissance Units, and that he had nothing to do with it.

"After some convincing he had me driven to the Province Interrogation Center.

"At the PIC there were two American civilians. I asked them if they were working for the CIA. I identified myself as representing CORDS from Headquarters MACV and on assignment from Colby. They looked at each other and admitted that they were."

"Unbelievable," said Earl.

"When I got back to Saigon I told Brown about it, but he dismissed it as isolated acts in war time. What do you think? I think I should write a memo, or whatever you want to call it, and tell what I found out about the CIA and send it to someone, I don't know who."

"Yeah," said Earl in his brash way. "Tell it to the world. Maybe it would help stop the war. Send it to Nixon. Send it to the *New York Times* and to the Anti-War Movement.

Actually, you should send it to Kissinger; after all he is Colby's boss."

I said, "Yeah that's right. That should get some attention."

Earl thought for a second and said, "Whose name would you put on it? Would you put *your* name on it? You'd have to send it anonymously if you wanted to keep your job, or your life for that matter."

I said, "I don't know – yeah definitely anonymous."

Earl said, "Go ahead and send it."

"Tough decision," I said. Earl nodded his head.

CHAPTER 5

Saturday as usual I rode my bike to work. When I arrived at my desk there were two well-dressed men standing by my desk with Carl. They introduced themselves to me and asked to see some recent papers I had written. It was obvious that these were agents from "The Company." I showed them some documents with my statistical analyses but they wanted to see some regarding the Phoenix program. For these, I had to go to the safe, which was located on the other side of the office. On the way back to my desk I overheard the two agents discussing the technical papers on my desk. I slowed down my walk to hear what they were saying.

"Do you understand this shit?" said one of the CIA men puzzling over the mathematical symbols. "Hell no," said the other.

I had to make an effort to remove the beginning of a smirk on my face. Were these the best our CIA could find? The agency had sent these two "intelligence experts" to investigate. I thought it was a bit frightening that the country would have to depend on such types for its national security.

When Carl heard that I had shown the agents some documents, he was visibly upset and, after the agents had left, made his cares known.

"He gave them some confidential information," he complained to one of the army majors. But the major said, "I'm sure whatever he gave them was OK."

At this rebuke, Carl spun angrily around on his heel and departed.

I wondered why these CIA guys had come to our office. Did they come only to *my* desk? I asked Carl but he said he was informed by Mike that they wanted some info about Phoenix. Was this related to my talk with Brown?

Later, there was a "General Meeting" in the CORDS Conference room. Two of the army majors had just returned from briefing President Thieu on HES-70 and he had put his stamp of approval on it. The new HES-70 was supposed to be an improvement over the old system in that the adviser answered the questions and did not rate the hamlet himself as in the old HES.

In the evening at the villa Ted came home with two red pepper plants. We carried the pots of plants upstairs to the roof. The maids were laughing at us. Ted was always pulling some weird deal.

On my way to work by bicycle the next morning, I almost got run over by an American tank that was maneuvering into place.

In the evening at dinner there was a rat behind the door to the lounge. Ted hit the glass door with his fist and it scampered away before the maids could get it.

Later in the night the usual flares could be seen from the villa roof off to the northeast. The people in the apartment building across Cong Ly lean out of their windows to stare.

At the villa, it seems that Ted had lost some of his clothes. He put up the following note:

TO: VILLA RESIDENTS

FROM: *Ted (Room 2)*

The following items were submitted for laundering never to return. Perhaps they were reissued to someone else who would be so kind as to return them.

One athletic supporter, wide waist band, size medium.

One large beach towel with multicolored figure of Neptune wearing shades. Impaled upon his fork are three signs:

1) LOVE, 2) PEACE, 3) NOW.

As for me, I have not been issued additional items, but I did receive one pair of white boxer shorts which are several sizes too large. Could it be that someone has a similar pair of smaller size which might be mine?

Ted had bought a funeral wreath at the local market and hung it up on his door. The maids were quite puzzled.

Next day, it was very hot and humid. I cycled downtown to Ramuncho's, a good restaurant with air conditioning. I went in and sat by a window. It was good to be out of the searing heat of Saigon.

As the restaurant specialized in French cuisine I thought I'd order a *Crêpe Suzette* and coffee. The clientele were French; in particular I noticed a family consisting of the bearded husband in his 40's, his wife, and his young son and daughter. From my table I could hear the mellow sounds of the French language. The whole "troupe" brought to mind the Swiss Family Robinson. The Alpine pictures on the walls added a further touch – the family fit the restaurant's motif.

The waiters, dressed in white frocks tied with red sashes, scurried around attempting to look efficient. I had to laugh at their bungling attempts to light the little fires under the crêpes.

After the pleasant meal and feeling cooler, I got back on my bike to get some breeze while cruising around sightseeing. From my bike I could observe the city and its people far better than from the interior of a moving car. Also the people seem to admire you for putting yourself in a more humble position. Sometimes the cyclo drivers look at me, fascinated, nod their heads and give me a big approving smile, flashing rows of teeth like a gold watch band.

How bizarre it was to look into those shops that make coffins and funeral ornaments. They were always wide open in the front. Inside, coffins were stacked against the walls and children scamper about, playing happily among them.

In the evening I walked over to the *Institut Français* to see a film. The Institute is located off noisy Hai Ba Trung. The narrow streets around the Institute are made even darker by tall, thick trees on both sides. There's the Grall Hospital up on the left, its cross glowing in the night. Then continuing around the corner to the right – a little downhill, a woman is selling sandwiches from a pushcart. On top of this cart there's a little candle or two – maybe even a small kerosene lamp whose inviting shadows flicker over the golden loaves of French bread. When I stopped to buy a small baguette for 10P the girl was preparing a sandwich with slices of meat, onions, peppers, and tomatoes for a Vietnamese soldier sitting on his bicycle. All is quiet and peaceful here in this oasis from the war.

Women, children, and old people sit, lie or squat around small lamps; one large family is seated around a table, comfortably chatting, moving chopsticks over bowls of rice. An old woman stirs soup in a pan over a fire. I walk through the darkened quarter, past gardens and silent houses.

Many times as I rode through Saigon I would notice the *Institut Pasteur* and wondered what they did there. In the paper was an article about this famous institute. It told the story of one incident that occurred there.

As the nurse prepared the syringe for the inoculation, the 20-year-old man suddenly leapt up in a fit of terror. He ran frantically around the medical room, jerking and gesticulating. The nurse watched helplessly as he finally sought out a corner and cowered, shaking in abject fear. Too late for the injection now. He would be dead within two days.

He had come too late to the Pasteur Institute Center for the Prevention of Rabies. Had he arrived for the inoculations immediately after he had been bitten by a mad dog, he would be alive today. Usually, without treatment, the victim dies within 48 hours. The number of people bitten by dogs in Vietnam is about 10,000 each year.

Dogs are commonly kept in Vietnam as watchdogs. In Saigon alone there are an estimated 20,000. As a point of interest, the Viet Cong kill many dogs in the countryside, not because of rabies but fear that the dogs will give away their nighttime movements.

Saigon's Center was established in 1891 by a French physician, Dr. Calmette, and now has a staff of one doctor, two medical students, a nurse, and four staff members.

On the way to work next morning I got only as far as Hien Vuong and Pasteur when I felt – then looked down and saw – that I had a flat tire and had to stop at a little fix-it "shop" on a corner. This consists usually of a man and his son or just a couple of kids with an old pushcart containing tire repair tools. Amazing how they can fix things somehow with little scraps of material. At night the flames from little burners they use to heat-seal inner tube patches produce a ghostly scene with flickering light and shadowy figures. The fires light up the whites of the boys' eyes against the rest of them – all black and smudged.

A policeman who had been standing around came up to me and started poking at the lock and chain of my bike and asked me how much I had paid for it. He asked if I had a key for the lock. What did this man want? When I opened my wallet to pay the fix-it man, the cop peered into the wallet, pointed to and touched an MPC note. It was incredible how the Vietnamese don't mind touching people or their belongings.

Someone at the company villa had heard that four Americans in Saigon had eaten watermelon and were fatally poisoned. A warning was passed around at MACV by memo with the heading: "Rush."

That evening, the Vietnamese maids served watermelon for dessert. I kidded Hue #2 that it was poisoned, and did not eat one. Up on the roof artillery sounds are louder than usual. It's a clear, starry night, balmy and breezy. The moon is in its first quarter and lies on its back like a bowl.

It was just announced on the radio that a bomb had exploded in the toilets of the Rex movie house; no known casualties. This is the second bombing of a movie house in less than two weeks. That, along with the watermelon poisoning, ambush of a civilian convoy a couple of days ago near Long Binh, and infiltration of VC into Saigon as "White Mice" (Vietnamese military police, as their uniforms are white) make one feel a bit uncomfortable.

Our work at MACV was reported in the *Stars and Stripes* headlines:

New System 'More Objective'

CORDS Changes Hamlet Evaluations

More people were becoming aware of what we were doing.

The French sporting club, called *Le Cercle Sportif Saigonnais*, was very prestigious. It had tennis courts, swimming pool, and an excellent restaurant. I had made formal application to join it and a coworker from MACV sponsored me. After the admission interview they told me that I would be accepted, and several days later I received an official letter in the mail at HQ confirming this. They were still writing in French.

Once in a while when I look out the window on the other side of our offices at Headquarters I see the sun shining. It seems hard to believe as we are shut up in here for most of the daylight hours.

Yesterday in Cholon I bought a Chinese signature stamp with my name phonetically written in Chinese characters. At work I let it be known by stamping it on a route slip. They all got a big kick out of it.

Weather is in the low 90s these days but cooler in the evenings; that is, down to low of 73-75. I keep the overhead fan on low speed all night and just one sheet over me.

A water pipe in front of the villa had broken, so the maid had to wheel in a heavy earthenware pot, nearly three feet high, from which I had to scoop out water with a plastic dipper to take a bath, make coffee or flush the toilet.

At noon Roger and I went to the airport for Chinese noodle soup. It wasn't the greatest restaurant around but it was close and we could watch the planes and people. A GI was leaving, going home; he and his Vietnamese girlfriend were embracing for the last time, saying their goodbyes. A big Pan Am 707 was looming outside on the tarmac. Roger laughed and said she's crying. "Don't laugh, it's not funny," I said, trying to be sympathetic. Roger admitted I was right and that he had felt the same way when his girlfriend had left. "It's too bad that Vietnamese girls get into situations like this," Roger said. "The guys always leave some day."

In the evening, as I was pedaling my bike back from work and got near my street I saw these two "cowboys," or young hoodlums, on a Honda behind me. I could see them eye my watch and gold band and laugh, then drift back and follow me. I continued down the heavily-traveled street and purposely did not turn into my own dark street. I continued on a few blocks to Dakao and turned left on a wide one-way street. They were still behind me; I could hear the "putt-putt" of their motorbike. I quickly made a U-turn and rode back down the one-way street the wrong way, no problem on a bicycle. They looked surprised at first. Then as I pedaled back to turn on my street, I felt in my bones that they had somehow whipped around through an alley and had caught me again. Sure enough, as I turned left onto my dark side street, I heard that little putt-putt sound and they pulled up beside me at arm's length. The boy on back reached out and just got a finger under the watchband when I let out a big karate yell and lashed my left arm out at them. This caused them to panic and the Honda wobbled back and forth as they picked up speed. Just then, another Honda came toward them from the right on a collision course. Calmly I kept pedaling and, while I was thinking "Wouldn't it be great if they collided," it happened. The cowboys veered way to the left to avoid the oncoming Honda then crashed into it and both went hurtling into the air. Justice was swift. As I rode up on my bicycle they were getting up off the ground. I yelled at them and pretended to start chasing them. They ran off in terror, eyes wide open in fright. They were only 14 or so. No one was really hurt in the accident but all in all it was a little adventure. I had also thought of the commercial on the military radio station AFVN (American Forces Vietnam Network):

Cowboys and your valuables don't mix, don't try to mix them.

Next evening I cycled over to the *Institut Français* to see the movie "Fanny" by Marcel Pagnol. The girl sitting next to me was wearing a perfume that smelled good. It was a sort of mysterious, sensual feeling sitting in a movie next to a woman when there's that electricity.

On my way out of the theater, I went to get my bike where I had left it outside. Alas, it was gone! I looked carefully at all the bikes and confirmed that mine was not among them. There was only one obvious conclusion: it had been stolen. I felt as though I'd lost a member of my family. There were many other bikes leaning against the wall but none of them sent the right familiar signals. Was I sure? I double checked; yes it's gone all right. Those three ARVN soldiers at the intersection are within sight of this spot. Could they have seen me just leave it there? I hadn't even pretended to lock it this time. I suddenly hated them, hated all Vietnamese. Everything was ugly. Yet, having had my valued property stolen, I felt more like a Vietnamese in that the bicycle is one of their most valuable possessions. One must save for months to be able to buy one. You need it even to get to and from work, to visit friends, to go out into the countryside on weekends. You polish the bike at the end of the day. At night it stands by your bed. Whoever lays hands on someone else's bicycle is the worst kind of thief.

I was almost in tears, suddenly realizing how attached I had become to that little $20 bicycle, bought partially for the reason that if it were stolen I wouldn't feel the loss. I could not sleep well that night.

Strangely I vacillated between "I'll never buy another one," and realizing I probably would. I hated to think of anyone else riding that bike; it had been my first one and I hadn't even taken pictures of myself on it yet.

When I got up in the morning, I was again rudely reminded of the theft as my bicycle wasn't in its usual place outside my door.

It was really hot. With no bike I had to walk, sweating profusely, down Tran Cao Van to the circle, then Duy Tan to Tu Do. I bought a copy of *Les Nouvelles du Dimanche* on the way to Ramuntcho's for lunch. It was advertised in the newspaper:

> *Ramuntcho's*
> *4E Le Loi Saigon, Across from the Rex.*
> *French food at its finest in authentic surrounding.*
> *Open from 11:00 am to the curfew time*

I had brought along a RAND Document to read titled *Origins of the Insurgency in South Vietnam 1954-1960: The Role of the Southern Vietminh Cadres.*

It was cool inside the restaurant, the air conditioner keeping the temperature just right. But then someone leaving the restaurant had not closed the door on their way out. A waiter moved quickly, his sandals shuffling along the tile floor, to thwart the offending blast of hot air, closing the door as though the fires of hell would blow in.

The people at the tables all had iced drinks in front of them. It was very quiet outside of the restaurant since the heat kept most people off the streets. The strong rays of the sun made walls of buildings resemble white frosting on a wedding cake, and blinding diamonds of reflected light pierced off the chrome strips on cars.

The sidewalks reflected the shimmering midday heat like the inside of an oven. "Mad dogs and Englishmen," those crazy enough to be outdoors, were a movie in slow motion.

In the small, rare corners of precious dark shade, were huddled amorphous squatting, chattering, laughing peasants. Even small children, also not in abundance in this normally-crowded section, seemed to have no energy for running. Sweat streaked down one's face and had to be flicked away using the thumb as a kind of windshield wiper.

After lunch, I decided to brave the heat and left the cool of the restaurant, found a taxi whose driver was not sleeping, and went along the main road to Cholon. I had bought my first bicycle in Cholon over two months ago but this time I found a new shop called "Le-Tan" at 8-10 Minh Mang Street. The brand name on the bike was "Sterling," made in China.

The owner of the bicycle shop was in purple pajamas with black dots. The bike cost 5,500P including generator, headlight, big tail light and a good tune up. Also, 200P for a lock (red plastic-covered cable). While waiting I sat down to read my French newspaper. One of the two boys working on the bike said,

"You Français?"

"No," I said. "American."

I got up to walk around but when I returned was surprised to see that my chair had been taken by an old woman. After I had been standing for a minute she unexpectedly picked up a stool that I hadn't noticed and set it down solidly with a flourish. I smiled broadly and "saluted" her informally as a "Thank You" and we smiled at each other.

It felt good to have wheels again but it just wasn't as good as my first one, a little smaller I think. Now I lock it everywhere.

In the evening I went to *La Cigale* in Dakao. Had pepper steak and tomato salad. Singers there with typical imitation American style. The Vietnamese singers' faces were pretty but character-less. There was more character in the face of a servant girl who was unobtrusively making her way back to the kitchen.

An official notice was passed around warning about off-limit areas; of course this just encouraged more customers, and guys would make copies of the accompanying maps.

OFF LIMITS AREAS

a. Sir's Tailor Shop, 119 Tran Hung Dao, Saigon
b. Unnamed Tailor Shop, 323 Dong Khanh, Cholon
c. Those stalls, stands, shacks or other facilities located adjacent to the RMKBRJ Motor Pool perimeter fence at USAT Newport
d. The Everest Hotel, 133 Tran Hung Dao, Saigon
e. "100-P" Alley which is the area bordered by Vo Tanh Street, Truong Minh Ky, Nguyen Minh Chieu, and Ngoc Hoa
f. "200-P" Alley which is that portion of Vo Di Nguy Street directly across from the rear gate of MACV Annex
g. The "Grass Shack." Area which is adjacent to Camp Davies
h. The Wooden Pier Area between the Saigon river and the unnamed road bordering the northern perimeter of Camp Davies and extending for a distance of approximately 50 yds. in an east-west direction, commonly called Rila Pier and all shacks, buildings, and structures located on or adjacent to this pier
i. "Soul Kitchen" 268/16 Truong Minh Ky, Gia-Dinh/Saigon
j. Capitol Hotel/Chiefs Club, 41 Bui Vien Street, Saigon
k. Dynasty Store, 31 Tu Do Street, Saigon
l. Building located at #19 Phu Kiet Street, Saigon

I was concerned that my money changing shop was on the list. Was the Dynasty Store my black market place? If so I would have to find a new place to change money. I went to Tu Do looking for number 31 and was relieved to see that it was not my shop.

After changing money I continued down Tu Do to the waterfront and had a refreshing iced tea in the My Canh floating restaurant on Bach Dang Quay as I longingly watched a Lykes Line freighter sounding its horn, pulling slowly around the first bend in the Saigon River.

CHAPTER 6

The next morning I rode my new bicycle the usual five miles to MACV through an insane rush of vehicles: old French Renault taxis, low-slung, black Citroën sedans, over-sized American cars, motorbikes, scooters, pedal cyclos, and motor-driven "cyclo-mais." Add to this the army deuce and a halfs, Military Police (MP) jeeps, and even flat-bed trucks. Dodging among all these vehicles were women in conical straw hats balancing long bamboo poles with baskets at each end.

The rattling, fuming flow of traffic with clouds of white exhaust smoke spewing out of this incredible mixture of vehicles was unimaginable. The motorbikes, scooters, and bicycles swerved around anything in their way. Accidents were a common occurrence. In a traffic jam, drivers would lean on their horns, some even attempting to get ahead by driving up over the sidewalk – whatever it took to move on. Others passed using the opposite lanes, causing ferocious head to head encounters. The jarring cacophony of hundreds of horns beeping was a constant irritant.

The Lambretta 3-wheelers were flimsy vehicles with one wheel in front and two in back, and so were very unstable when going around curves. They always carried full loads of peasants who sat inside facing each other on hard benches. Nearly every day we saw scattered wrecks where they had flipped over at an intersection. There was blood on the street and sandals were scattered as passengers had tried to scramble away.

The next day was Sunday, my day off. I went to the well-known Vietnamese-American Association, or *Hoi Viet My*, in Vietnamese. This was a combined American/Vietnamese cultural school on Mac Dinh Chi. It presented a range of events showing Vietnamese culture to Americans and American culture to Vietnamese, with plays, concerts, art exhibitions, lectures and language classes. There were some 15,000 students enrolled, mostly Vietnamese trying to learn English. Students and ex-students varied in background from President Thieu, office workers, bar girls, cabinet ministers (mini-sters to mini-skirts) and, it was assumed, VC agents. Why not? It was a cheap way for them to learn English.

I then wandered around a USO art exhibit on Nguyen Hue, and an open market on Hai Ba Trung. On Cong Ly there was an old school, the *Lycée Marie Curie*, from the French colonial period that was still functioning. I noticed on the wall out front there was a list giving the names of those accepted. Many French names were on that list.

Cong Ly, together with its northern extension Cach Mang, was one of Saigon's longest streets and led from the eastern part of downtown all the way to Tan Son Nhut International Airport and Headquarters MACV.

It felt good to be outside during the middle of the day after so many hours cooped up indoors at MACV. This was supposed to be the cool season but the temperature was in the mid or upper 80's with high humidity. Walking only a few blocks one was dripping with sweat – I scraped it off my forehead with my thumb. I hated to think what it would be like in the hot season starting in April or May. At that time, they told me, a walk downtown (about five-six blocks) was "out of the question."

I had learned a little Vietnamese, and also the numbers. Instead of just telling the taxi driver to go to Cong Ly, I could say the street number in Vietnamese as well. However, before this added precision, I would wait and when I saw the ESSO station I would tell him to stop. Now, though, as soon as the driver got to Hai Ba Trung, he slowed down to a crawl and began looking at the numbers.

At dinner that evening Paul was telling us about some of his adventures in Saigon. Nearly every day he was at his trusty Smith Corona electric typewriter pounding out letters, one after the other, then promptly sending them across the Pacific back home. Material for this voluminous correspondence was often supplied in the form of on-the-spot notes he nearsightedly makes on tiny scraps of paper at the drop of a local anecdote.

Paul was a character, big, crew-cut, early fifties. "I'm just a country boy, just an ignorant country boy," he laughingly said of himself. This confession came with every sad story of local bar girls relieving him of a few thousand P.

There had been an attempt to break into the villa during the night by some men who had tried to enter by climbing up to the roof. But the guard had spotted them and chased them away. Perhaps even more annoying than the attempted break-in was that there was no running water for my shower.

The next evening Paul was bringing a girlfriend home to the villa and as he opened the door to his room, he was confronted with the sight of Ted sitting on the bed watching TV, "guarding" the villa with a carbine on his lap. Paul's girlfriend made herself at home, went to take a shower but as often happened there was no water.

Ted, not being of such a literary bent or not having anyone to write to, often went "downtown" to the girlie bars on Tu Do. This was his wont while in town and not on a field trip. The *California Bar* had been definitely put down and classified "number 10" (the worst) after a series of incidents in which both Paul and Ted had been duped into dropping "beaucoup P" (lots of Piasters) for a girlfriend and seeing no one show up at the villa afterwards. Finally, Ted met with success at a "new" bar. In fact he had two gals and told me that he even knocked on my door to show the wealth but I was asleep and did not answer.

Christmas at MACV there was a sharing of presents from back home in the States. It was a much more relaxed atmosphere. Most of the packages contained some kind of food such as fruitcake. It was hard to believe it was Christmas when the temperatures were in the upper 80's. There was a Christmas party at the villa but not as many people as at the Thanksgiving one.

Frank Wadleigh

The local papers would often have humorous articles:

Vietnam Guardian

LOOKING AROUND

Pinchers Pinched

70 young men were arrested when they were turned in by women for public indecency. Most of the women complained that in the push of the throngs on crowded streets, they had their nipples pinched and other parts of their bodies 'violated.'

On a more sober note, Vice President Ky made a statement to the Press:

The Vietnam Guardian:

Ky: 1970 will decide fate of Vietnam

He also said that a coalition government in Saigon would be formed "over my dead body."

The papers are full of news and retrospectives on the past year.

Dec 31, 1969 *The Saigon Post* front page:

Happy New Year!

Paris Parley Still Up In Air As Year Ends
Thieu Rules Out New Tet Offensive

GOOD-BY (sic) TO THE 60's

Welcome To The 70's

US To Draft 19,000 Men

74

Men Of The Year:

EXPLORATION Neil Armstrong
PUBLICITY Tiny Tim
PUBLIC RELATIONS Spiro Agnew
POLITICS Richard M. Nixon
COMMENTARY William F. Buckley Jr.
NOTORIETY Lieut. William F. Calley Jr.
TELEVISION Walter B. Cronkite
ACTING Dustin Hoffman
FAME Aristotle Onassis
HUMOR Groucho Marx
CONSUMPTION Ralph Nader
MARTYRDOM Ho Chi Minh
BUSINESS Howard Hughes

New Year's Eve

I just went home on the bus, had dinner with one of the guys at the villa, went up to the roof and we played darts and drank beer. I spotted a chopper landing on the Embassy roof. It was Vice President Agnew on one of his so-called "fact-finding trips." Agnew would periodically fly over to Vietnam, take a look around and report back to Nixon that everything was fine.

Next day there was a big meeting on HES-70 in the afternoon. During the boring meeting, I was thinking of looking around for an inexpensive room. The only things keeping me at the villa were that it was convenient, and the meals were good. Earl would always distribute special cards to guys who had stayed a long time at the villa; they were made members of a special *Celibacy and Chastity Marching Society.*

In those days when anyone wanted to make a phone call to the States it was necessary to call MARS (Military Affiliated Radio Service). This was a group of amateur radio operators who cooperated with the military to relay calls between Vietnam and various places in the States. Contact was very spotty. One had to put one's name on the list at 1830 and then wait for a good connection. It was amusing when a military guy was calling home and as they were saying goodbye, he would say, "Love you/over."

At HQ I received a memorandum that spelled out another attempt at tightening up the VCI reporting system. It was regarding the so-called "Big Mack Reporting System."

I ate lunch in town and then walked to a park just off Hong Thap Tu. It was a warm day, warmer than usual, and sweat ran down my face just from the effort of walking along the streets, strangling with people and choking with lethal blue and white exhaust fumes. I wandered into one of Saigon's parks with its tall, beautiful trees, shrubs, and grass that are such a contrast with most of Saigon. I sat on a bench to relax. As I began writing notes in my diary, a small boy approached, selling doughnuts that he carried on a big metal tray. They were twisted ones topped with an orange glaze. The boy gave the price as "Nam Dong" (5P). Smiling, I gave him the small coin and the boy handed me a doughnut that he held in a scrap of Chinese newspaper.

After I had finished eating the doughnut and started to write again, I was startled by a few stones that landed suspiciously close to me. I looked up and noticed that a small group of Vietnamese soldiers clad in shorts who were scrubbing their clothes at the fountain, were regarding me with a mixture of curiosity and, it seemed, dislike. Funny thing is, long periods of time would go by when no one seemed to pay attention to me, then suddenly I felt very conspicuous.

The park now seemed exclusively Vietnamese and I felt like an intruder. But I was determined to soak up all the greenery I could. Dark clouds were covering half of the sky and rain seemed imminent, although the rest of the sky was still completely blue.

I decided to leave before it started to rain and walked quickly over to Ted's place. Both of us then went to Paul's room in an apartment building on Pasteur. Paul paid $150 "green" for his place every month. He sent the cash to the owner's sons who lived in the States. In addition to this he paid 30,000P a month for his Vietnamese girlfriend.

Back at the villa that evening, Ted went out to the *Pink Pussycat*, making sure his "beautiful" Chinese girl showed up. He'll go to Vung Tau with her tomorrow.

Being so far away in Vietnam and completely cut off from all possibility of seeing anyone back home seemed to release the mind from pressures of living with them in the present and allowed the past to rise again in memory, as it were, no longer constantly being overwritten by daily contact and new experiences with the people involved.

Tomorrow is Tet, the Chinese and Vietnamese New Year. Everything is already crowded, traffic is almost at a standstill and everything is closed. We still have to work though. The "Year of the Dog" starts at midnight. Months before Tet, businessmen get ready for the expected surge in sales. Practically every family buys large quantities of food for the holidays, not only to eat but to place on their ancestors' altars. During this season the Vietnamese enjoy many special dishes that they do not prepare at any other time of the year.

Everyone dresses up for the holidays and, according to tradition, he who goes out on the first day of Tet wearing old clothing is looked down on as being in a state of poverty. The family may go to the pagoda to burn incense and pray for a prosperous new year. They take home a bud from a plant or tree as a symbol of happiness.

Going into downtown Saigon during the Tet holidays one has to thread and duck one's way down the sidewalk between and under the stalls that are spread out in profusion as far as you can see. Scribes set up tables on the sidewalks and are busy writing letters for illiterates, while calligraphers fashion gold Chinese characters on huge scrolls with messages for Tet.

According to Vietnamese custom, everyone has his birthday on New Year's Day, no matter when he was born. People could be seen carrying apricot branches home. In a restaurant, there were tangerine plants in pots on either side of the entrance. In the words of the little brochure formerly handed out by the Vietnam National Tourist Office:

In Saigon, the festival is particularly brilliant. The sidewalks are flooded with flower stands, and boulevards are adorned with long, luminous garlands. Houses are especially decorated for the occasion with flowering branches, and for at least 3 days running, from the eve of the Tet, firecrackers are set off everywhere.

In a few days the Tet holidays were over and the villa maids were back so we have clean clothes again, and for the first time in a week we can get a full breakfast instead of just self-service bread, butter and jam. There are only four of us at the villa now.

In the morning when my little Japanese alarm clock rings I quickly shut it off and turn on the radio to AFVN with its "Gooood Morning Vietnam." Paris Peace talks are still in the news.

HES-70 was slowly being approved for adoption by all the various military and civilian agencies: Colby, General Abrams, and Ambassador Bunker. Then it had to go to President Thieu and finally to the National Security Council in Washington. There was tremendous pressure on advisers to increase hamlet security ratings.

The American Embassy issued a notice on the subject of personal security measures. This very comprehensive list consisting of dozens of warnings was typical of the American Embassy in its ludicrous conservatism and occasional downright absurdities. Just a few of them:

AMERICAN EMBASSY, SAIGON VIETNAM

SUBJECT: Personal Protective Security Measures

Exercise extreme care in the selection and use of public transportation, especially taxis, cyclos and motor cars. Avoid traveling alone. Employ the "buddy system."

If an explosion of a VC mine or charge occurs, anticipate a second explosion to follow. The VC usually plant a second explosive device.

If authorized a weapon, use it only to safeguard your life. Indiscriminate firing may only attract enemy and friendly fire.

US Military Police
Attachment: Instructions to servants.

The maids had taken over my room at the company villa. I was moved upstairs and had to share a bathroom with the guy next door and his girlfriend. Also they will put offices on the entire third floor, so there'll be even less privacy than before. It was time to move out.

I examined the list of rooms to rent in *The Saigon Post*. There were two that seemed promising, and in the evening I went to look at them. The first room on the list turned out to be in a noisy commercial area, but the next one was a converted garage attached to a villa in one of the better residential areas near the American Embassy. I told the Vietnamese couple who owned it that I would take it.

Next day, three guys from the office, including Ted from the villa, helped me move to my new room. "Evening no dinner, drunk in Dakao," I wrote in my diary.

On the back of the rent receipt for the room was the following note written by the Vietnamese landlord in English. He must have copied it from one that applied to a shop.

THE CONDITION OF RENTING HOUSES

1. Money renting houses must pay before every month.
2. If you don't want to rent more, you must write the letter to the shopkeeper before 15 days about 15th and 30th in the month.
3. No renting houses allowed for the others.
4. Sirs, never put on the waste materials in the W. C. because you use some hard materials in the W. C. you can't use it more.
5. If you want to repair the house, you must speak with the shopkeeper.

From its days as a garage, the room had a corrugated metal roof that turned into a deafening echo chamber when the hard monsoon rains banged down. As the Vietnamese couple owning the villa spoke French, I had no communication problem. The maid, however, spoke neither English nor French.

The room was rather long and narrow as you'd expect for a former garage, and was partitioned into a "bedroom" at one end, and "lounge" on the other, by a simple cloth curtain and a bookcase. Behind the bedroom was a tiny bathroom with toilet, sink, and shower that rarely had hot water.

I bought an electric Teflon frying pan at the PX and made instant coffee by putting water in a small pot and setting it on the pan.

The bed was a little too short and a little too hard, just a mattress on top of wood slats. There was no air conditioning, only two overhead fans. Opposite the bed was a wardrobe, one door of which nearly always fell off when I opened it. In the lounge I set up what Ted would call my "altar" – a framed oil painting of an old man on the wall above a small table. On the table sat a blue china bowl containing sand in which I had stuck several incense sticks. As usual in non air-conditioned rooms in the orient, there were no real windows, just "breeze block" – a kind of large, latticed brick with shaped openings to let through any possible cool outdoor air. The two ceiling fans are controlled by a variable-speed knob on the wall. In the high position, needed during the hottest nights, the wind from the fan over the bed would cause the sheet to lift and flap over my sleeping body. I would leave the fans on when I left for work, but the maid invariably turned them off, so that everything in the room soon became moldy and mildewy. Books, attaché case, half-finished coffee, all would turn a primordial white-green. Thus one could easily pick up a bad cough from floating spores. Cockroaches scurry about, especially at night, and the lizard-like geckos scoot over the walls.

According to the radio, several jeeps were blown up yesterday in Saigon. There was an MP/QC checkpoint at Phan Dinh Phung and Mac Dinh Chi tonight and their whistles could be heard. The sounds of artillery are louder over here than they had been at the company villa.

The next day I stopped by the old villa. Ted was there, back from Bangkok with his new Vietnamese "wife." He had bought a punching bag there and was showing it off to her, feigning the look of a real boxer.

Next morning I woke up a bit late, about seven. Fortunately the water was on again. I had a quick cup of coffee and then rode my bike to MACV.

"I'm glad to see that some of us is rubbing off on you," said one of he majors, holding up my memo on non-evaluated hamlets. With a slight smile, he read out loud, "Questions will be answered by the number." We laughed, then he says, "Good memo, thank you." It was good to get some compliments from the military.

I cycled back to the room after work and as I walked across the courtyard, I noticed two 20P notes lying on the ground. My first thought was to keep them but then I decided to give them to the villa owner who I call "Monsieur." I knocked on the door of the main part of the villa where the family lives. "Monsieur" came rapidly to the door. Handing him the notes I said in French "I found these on the ground." He smiled and said, "Merci bien."

I wanted to take a shower but there was no water. I told the owner and the maid brought me a small bucketful for a bath. When I was done and on my way out, the family's 12-year-old son ran out and opened the gate for me. I took this gesture to mean that they had appreciated my returning their money.

I walked up to Ly's bar in Dakao and soon after I arrived Carl came in. We talked to some of the girls including the one we called "Too Short." She said to me, "I see eyes, nose, mouth, good." We decided to check out Flora's next door to meet Earl who said he'd be there. We ordered our beers at the bar and then a new girl came over to us. She was by far the most attractive, intelligent and charming of all the girls we had seen there or at any other bar in Saigon. She was distinctly different from the run-of-the-mill bar girls, from a much higher class and did not really fit in with the others in background and manner. We sat in a booth with her. Aside from her beauty, one of the first things I noticed about her was her apparently sincere smile. Although shy, when she talked she was very animated and would tilt her head with a come-on smile.

Her facial expressions were a mix of energy and naïveté, sometimes the look and giggle of a child, full of freshness and youth. Her complexion was a clear very light brown and her voice was gentle and sweet.

Her jet black hair was longer than most of the girls' and from time to time as she was speaking she would brush away a strand that was hanging over her shoulder. Perhaps it was a calculated move? Her hair framed a face that was a very pleasing oval. Her eyes sparkled. Her nose was a bit "pug," as with all Vietnamese.

As she speaks, her eyebrows arch up to accentuate a point. She looked at you directly, throwing her beauty into your face. The lips and chin show a determination, maybe even stoic asceticism.

This young woman was Thanh. When she told us her name I noticed that she pronounced it "Tahn" without the "th" sound, and with the "a" as in "father." We talked with her quite a long time while she sipped her "Saigon Tea." She seemed to be interested in me in particular for some reason. She even asked me where I live. As the lights flickered and went out, indicating that curfew time had arrived, she whispered in my ear, "You must come here tomorrow."

"Yes," I said, "I will be here tomorrow night."

At closing time, you could hear the Hondas starting up their motors ready to offer the bar patrons a ride home. I recalled the advice in a brochure on Saigon:

Residents and visitors must use only licensed taxi cabs and cyclos. You must remember that it is illegal to use a two-wheeled vehicle for hire. Therefore do not accept the offers of motor scooter drivers who will ask you where you want to go. This is illegal, and in many instances these people will try to cheat you.

There are a lot of such rules in Saigon but few are followed. Whenever I left Flora's to go home I always took the Honda whose driver said, "*Comment allez-vous?*" ("How are you?") and "*Merci, monsieur.*" He charged only 50P, was friendly and did not "cheat" – did not try to ask for more money.

The next day at MACV all I could think about was seeing Thanh again. When I got home that evening there was an envelope under my door. Inside was a hand-written note:

My Dear –
I have missing you very much.
I can not wait for you anymore.
please, come to see me.
Hurry up.
as always,
(signed) Thanh

P.S. Please, Do not let me wait for you so long because I will death.

How to find her? I went to Flora's but she was not there. I told one of the girls that Thanh was looking for me. She said she would take a message to her. The next day was Sunday and my day off, so perhaps she would come to my room.

The next morning she did come to my room but with her best friend Lien. They told me they would go for lunch then come back. After a brief conversation they left.

At one o'clock, there was no sign of her. I thought this was not unusual as in the Far East one is not pressed for time. Patience is a key word. If you ask an ordinary Vietnamese at what time such and such an event takes place, you would likely receive the following answer: "That happens when the sun is on the top of the bamboo tree."

I went out in front of the villa looking for her. In a few minutes I spotted her half a block down Tran Quy Cap slowly walking towards me with that harmonic sway of the hips and curvaceous figure. She was dressed in a brown ao dai that swished along majestically as she walked.

She had a very straight posture, thrusting out her chest as she walked.

When she arrived in front of the villa, I joked with her and we both laughed as I playfully picked her up in my arms and carried her into the courtyard. I then shut the gate and we strolled arm in arm to my room.

Inside, it seemed to me impossible that I was now actually alone with her. It surprised me that I was a bit nervous. "Do you want some tea?" I asked her; the irony of the question not occurring to me at that moment.

"Yes, please."

"Who is the girl?" she asked teasingly. I had stuck a photo of an American girl in the frame of a Vietnamese black velvet painting that I had hung on the wall.

"Oh, just a friend," I said, matter-of-factly, trying to minimize the importance of this girl.

She laughed, bending over at the waist, placing a hand on her thigh. The Vietnamese women have this kind of inhaling laugh and Thanh did this to the ultimate, I thought. She seemed to have mastered this feminine trait and often would place her hand over her mouth like a giggling school child. This childlike behavior of the bar girls was in odd contrast to their street smartness. Perhaps it stemmed from the idea that it was not polite, or not feminine, for a woman to show her teeth while laughing.

She sat on the edge of my bed to sip her tea. Her long jet-black hair hung down to the small of her back. Her seductive open mouth smile melted me. She did something to my head, as they say.

It seemed a bit of an awkward moment so I went to the door pretending to check on some noise in the front courtyard, then lit a few incense sticks. The acrid smoke curled upwards and when I turned around to look at her, she had undressed and was slipping into the bed, pulling the white sheet over her small, young body. She smiled provocatively at me.

After the love making, when she had finished dressing, she sat down on the bed again next to me. She suddenly became quite serious and said softly, "I am afraid for my brother."

"What?" I was completely taken aback.

"He is arrested by police. He is student at Saigon University and he protest war."

"They arrested him just for that?" It was like in the States, I suddenly thought.

"Yes, he is leader."

"But he is not VC, is he?"

"No, he only want peace, just like students in America. But he is arrested and will be tortured, like the others." She started to cry.

"I think you can save him," she said.

"What do you mean? How can I save him?"

"My brother is on list. You can change list."

"What list?"

"It is a list from Phuong Hoang."

"You mean Phoenix?" I had no idea what to say. Was this an act?

"I have something I must to tell you," she said, her face suddenly very serious but still radiant. "You know we do not meet by chance."

"What?"

"This is so hard to tell you. I must to do it for my parents and grandparents."

"Do what?"

"Somebody tell me to meet you."

"Who?"

"You not believe."

"Yes, just tell me."

"It was a man from your CIA."

I thought for a second and it dawned on me. Brown! So that's why he didn't listen to my accusations of the CIA.

I was hit by the double-barreled shock of this confession and the implications. It crossed my mind that I'd read that a Vietnamese girl hired by the CIA to spy for the Phoenix program was called a "Phoenix mistress."

"I tried to tell my boss about the Phoenix but he said it was not important. Now I know why he said that. So that's how you know that I am working on the computer lists for the Phoenix program and the lists of students against the war?"

"Yes, I am sorry. Will you try to get him off the list and out of prison?"

"I will try," I said, thinking that I would be entering dangerous ground. "What is your brother's name?"

"His name is Minh. Here, I will write it down for you. Please try. When can you do this?"

"I will find out how to do it. It may take some time."

"Let me know as soon as you can."

"I will. It won't be easy you know."

"I go now?" she asked softly.

As Earl would say later, she was "Part pixie, part schemer, with one never knowing how much to believe."

The poet John Donne had said:

In woman, so perchance milde innocence
A seldome comet is.

We got ready to leave and walked out to the street. Hailing a cyclo she said to me, "Please help him. I will come over tomorrow evening."

I watched the cyclo go slowly down the street and just stood there trying to take in what had just happened.

At this point I wanted once more to consult with my friend Earl, but he was now in the Delta so I would have to wait until he came to Saigon.

I had to figure out what to do. I wanted to find out if Thanh's brother was VC, and if not, then how to get him out of jail.

Confirming Thanh's story, it was announced in the papers that a two-week boycott will be launched by 6,000 students of the Saigon Medical College, initiating a general boycott by university and college students in the whole city, demanding the release of Tran Van Minh, president of the Saigon Students Association, and 39 other student activists arrested by the Saigon regime.

At MACV, I received a memo spelling out new VCI tracking procedures. It showed that the National Police (NP) would be more involved with the Phoenix program.

MACCORDS-PHX
SUBJECT: VCI Tracking System

An Arrest Report, which will be in machine-compatible, bio-data form indicating the VCI function(s) of the detainee, will be completed by the National Police (NP) agency effecting the arrest. A copy of the arrest report will be sent to DGNP/Saigon (Director General National Police) and a copy will go to the PIOCC (Province Intelligence and Operations Coordination Center) and be used as the basis for reporting a VCI captured on the monthly VCI Neutralization Report.

Concurrently, the NP will fingerprint the detainee and send the fingerprint card to DGNP where a search will be made at the National Identity Records Center (NIRC) to determine other data which may be on file which may add to the detainee's Offender Dossier.

The above procedures will allow for constant tracking of VCI detainees and will provide machine printouts to be used by the PHUNG HOANG/ PHOENIX Program agencies at all echelons to expeditiously determine the status of each VCI.

Signed X
COL, INF
Acting Director, PHOENIX

Since the National Police were now involved in the Phoenix program, this connection might enable me to talk with the director and see how to free Thanh's brother. The director was also a high official in the Central Intelligence Organization (CIO), the Vietnamese CIA. Obtaining such an interview would not be difficult given my new assignment on the Phoenix program.

CHAPTER 7

A meeting was set up with the Police Director at a "safe-house" in a residential section of the city. It was a villa only a short bike ride from my room on Tran Quy Cap.

The villa was a gigantic embassy-size, red-tile-roofed building, shaded by lush tropical trees and surrounded by the obligatory high wall topped with concertina wire and broken glass shards. When I pulled up on my bicycle it seemed really incongruous and caused great surprise and squelched amusement on the part of the guards.

The director is a youngish man, smiling easily. There is no outward appearance of a hardened top spy chief. He speaks fluent French, tinged with a Vietnamese accent. It is surprising how the French influence survives. There is no bitterness in speaking the language of the former colonialists. "I'm very happy to see you. Please take a seat," he said, smiling, and indicating that I should sit at the opposite end of the sofa from him.

There is an older Vietnamese woman loudly washing dishes in the kitchen just off the lounge. Why does she have to be doing this right now? I wondered.

I decided to begin directly.

"I have a question about the students who were recently arrested. I would like to find out if there are any records for the leader. His name is Tran Van Minh. I would like to know about his family, if he has brothers and sisters, what their names are, and what they do, etc. I am writing a report on possible VC or communist backing for the student anti-war protests."

"I know that there were some students arrested," he said. "I will look at our records and let you know the details you need tomorrow." He jotted down a reminder on a notepad.

"There are many students in the US who are protesting against the war and they are not communists. I have seen what is going on here in Vietnam and actually, I agree with them."

"Yes, I know," he said. My daughter is now living in America and is one of the anti-war protesters. Here in Saigon and everywhere in Vietnam, students are being arrested and tortured. I am not able to do anything about this within the present government. There are computer records where you are working at the CORDS that I do not have access to and unless these records are changed there is no way to help them."

"Perhaps we can work together. Actually I am trying to get this fellow Tran Van Minh released from prison and if I send you the details where his classification has been changed, then maybe you will be able to get him released?"

"Yes, we can work together on this but we must not let anyone know what we are doing. You will not tell anyone about this I hope."

"Of course not. I will send you the changed record of Minh and then you will see that he is released?"

"Yes. I know that Minh is not a communist and that he is a real patriot."

"It is very fortunate then that we can work together and that I have come to see you."

"Yes indeed. Please send me the new records as soon as possible."

"Thank you. Do you mind if I ask you some questions? I am not familiar with your background."

"Certainly, go ahead."

"Have you ever been associated with the American CIA?"

"I was trained by them some time ago."

"In Washington?"

"No, it was at a base in Hawaii. At the time it was strictly confidential."

"Was it the CIA who was teaching you?"

"They didn't tell us exactly, but we guessed that it was."

"What kinds of things did they teach you?"

"That is to say they reasoned like this, to combat communism, you have to know what communism is." His voice became stronger.

"Their methods?"

"Yes. We spent two months learning what communism is – the organization of the communist party, military security, all sorts of things. They were intelligence officers. I didn't know whether they were civilian or military officers. We didn't know anything; we only knew them by false names, like Mr. X. We were fairly sure they were officers in the CIA."

"How long were you there?"

"For six months."

"What year was it?"

"It was in 1960. You know, in those early years the Americans had no intention of becoming deeply interested in the affairs of Vietnam. They were just advisors."

"In the beginning."

"Yes, but that changed. During this time the army was organized by the American method and then the administration too."

"Six months in Hawaii and after that what did you do?"

"Afterwards, I was appointed Director of the Vietnamese CIO, the Vietnamese Central Intelligence Organization."

"This is the Vietnamese CIA?"

"Yes, it is in a way. This was at the time when the Vietnamese officers had a revolution in '63 and President Diem was killed. You know, this CIO is divided into two services, external security and internal security."

"Is it possible that Madame Nhu (wife of Ngo Dinh Nhu, President Diem's brother) was behind the assassination of President Kennedy since he was president at the time Diem was murdered?"

"No, it's too far for her, too far," he said, laughing. "You know, Madame Nhu was not actively involved in the intelligence activities. She didn't have many supporters so she could do nothing without Nhu or Diem, you know. She could do some low things, what we call 'dirty politics.' She came to the United States to plead the cause of Diem, when the world opinion condemned Diem for suppressing the monks and there was no freedom of belief or religion in Vietnam. Madame Nhu went to try to deny these stories. So already this was embarrassing for her, I can guarantee you that. I don't think the American information sources were very successful. I don't think they had very good knowledge about Vietnamese affairs. How do you find the Vietnamese people?"

"I don't think many Vietnamese, especially in the upper class, want to associate with Americans."

"That depends. I don't think the Vietnamese are especially reticent; I think they are naturally quite open. They are not taciturn like the French."

"Of course Americans aren't very welcome here are they?"

"Yes, that is because you have come to Vietnam a bit too late. Actually, before this, we had a lot of esteem for the Americans during the Diem regime. Until the coup against Diem. People said that if Diem was assassinated it was because the Americans had their hand in it. That's for sure. How should I say it? Many Vietnamese were unhappy about this intervention. We had much esteem and hope for Diem as a balance against communism. In North Vietnam they had Ho Chi Minh; in the south we had to have someone of the same caliber. But after the death of Diem it was finished. We blamed the Americans because they had intervened and the revolution led by the officers was successful because the Americans were behind it. If they had stood aside, these Vietnamese officers never would have dared to revolt. They're not courageous enough. That's definite. One hundred percent sure."

"What caused the Americans to be dissatisfied with Diem?"

"Oh, there were many causes. Mainly you have to understand who was this Ambassador (Henry) Cabot Lodge. He was an ambassador different from all other ambassadors."

"An aristocrat?"

"Yes, he was an aristocrat. A real snob – haughty. And he was up against President Diem who was of the same caliber. You know, in political affairs there are always multiple causes, small, multiple causes. If President Kennedy had been in his office that day, the revolution never would have taken place but he had gone on vacation and his adviser who was acting in his place was a man who really detested President Diem. I don't remember his name. He received the telegram from Cabot Lodge, OK? After he made his report, President Kennedy said, 'Oh, wait, wait!' But it was already done. The American intervention in this was kept very discrete, very, very secret. The head of the CIA, (John) McCone, was also not in his office that day. The next Monday morning when he returned to his office he said,

'What? Revolution in Saigon?' He knew nothing about it. There were many strange coincidences."

"And after Diem?"

"Oh, there were all sorts of revolutions. After Diem there was Minh, Big Minh. That was a very troubled period, very troubled."

"And Thieu, he was more or less installed by the Americans wasn't he?"

"Yes, a puppet, since he couldn't fight Nguyen Cao Ky – that's not easy, not easy. After the revolution in 1963 led by the Vietnamese officers the war became worse since the communists had now found a motive for fighting the war. It was, 'Chase the Americans out of Vietnam.' *Voilà.* The communists said, 'The Americans want to dominate Vietnam to make Vietnam a new colony. A sort of neo-colonialism, all sorts of things. Now you must fight the Americans to save your country.' So we fight the war to chase out the foreigners, or 'liberation' as the communists call it. The communists have spent a lot of money and effort on propaganda in the North. Propaganda, it's to fool all the people. The Vietnamese are not as communist as you think. They have been led by the communists, organized and led. They no longer had liberty of thought, or action or to eat or sleep. They were no longer free. You did only what the party or government told you to do and that's all. The communists went into South Vietnam for the express purpose of fighting the Americans. The patriots in the South were unhappy and dominated by the Americans."

I said, "It seems like it's easier to hate people like the Americans than it is to be against an idea like communism."

"Yes, because they didn't keep Diem. It's the fault of the government who didn't think to organize the people in Vietnam to lead a war against the communists. They were not free to act as they wanted since the Americans were there. The Vietnamese couldn't use American aid as they wished, they had always to get the agreement of the Americans."

"Why do Americans come to fight in Vietnam?"

"To fight communism. That's for sure."

"But that's the supposed cause. Is it the real reason?"

"The real reason? I think it's the real reason. Do you know why? Before, the Americans supported the Chiang Kai-shek regime in China, the nationalist regime. When the communists defeated Chiang the Americans had lost a long battle, an enormous battle. So what do they have to do now to remedy the situation? Occupy Vietnam immediately and put their foot in the huge continent of Asia."

"The domino theory?"

"Yes, since if the communists occupied China and then Vietnam it would be very dangerous so the Americans had to put their foot on Vietnamese soil. But how should they do this? This is why at first the Americans helped the French to regain Indochina. You know, the French after World War II were very poor, they could no longer support a war. They could only do so with American support – money and equipment. But after a while they changed their minds."

"Isn't it true that Ho Chi Minh after the First World War asked President Wilson for the independence of Vietnam from the French – and Wilson refused?"

"I'm not sure, because the war ended in 1918 and Ho Chi Minh was still young, you know. He came to France and was one of the founding members of the French Communist Party. After that, he went to Moscow for a long time. When Ho Chi Minh returned to Vietnam he had for some time the support of the Americans. He helped fight the Japanese and became master of Vietnam. The Americans went back also. I was there. There was an American mission, but I think the mission failed in its work – they couldn't get Ho Chi Minh to abandon his communist ideology, so the Americans abandoned him.

"Once the communist regime is propagated in the country, it's difficult to shake off. Because they have an extraordinary way of governing the people, you know.

"To really govern a people what do you have to do? What do you think? To really govern people – to dominate people, to direct people. What do you have to do according to you?"

"To direct them well?"

"To direct well, govern people well, lead people well. What do you have to do?"

"Do you mean in a communist country, or in a democratic country?"

"In any country," (laughs but is emphatic).

"I think it's education. To indoctrinate the people."

"No. Absolutely false."

"But I think that's very important."

"Not only false, but it's terribly false! Because we believed that and you too, and the democratic world also. The communists, you know, they are very close to reality. When it comes to governing people, directing people, they hold them by the stomach. That's it exactly. When you don't have bread in your stomach you can't do anything. You can't help obeying. If you don't obey, you won't get anything to eat that evening. If you go three days without eating, five days without eating you'll know pain. No doctrine, no ideas. Nothing at all. The stomach. He bore down on this by strongly enunciating each syllable of the French word for stomach (*l'estomac*). When one holds your stomach, you can't buy anything; you are so weak you can't even move. You can't do anything – no strikes, no discussion, you can't do anything at all, because you haven't eaten in a week. You're going to have a conference when you're starving? No way. The truth is there are two ways to look at things. The way of looking when you're rich and the way of looking at things when you are poor. It's different. When they hold the people, they hold them by their stomachs – all the people, even the poorest peasants. All food products are in the hands of the party. You work but the harvest goes to the party. The party gives you just enough to eat for a week and in three days you come back for your ration. You can't even give anything to your father who has no ration. If you have one piece of bread, or some rice, it's for you for three days, you can't share it with everyone or you'd starve.

"Do you understand what I'm saying? Do you agree? Do you agree or not? Maybe it's because you have never been hungry, but if you stay without eating for three or four days, you'll know what hunger is. But none of the Americans know what hunger is. No."

"Have you done it yourself?"

"In the wars, no. But I've seen, I've seen it, I've seen it."

"When was that?"

"That is to say, after the Japanese occupation we had two million people starve to death. Two million! Dead because they had nothing more to eat. Oh, it's terrible. It's a slow death, slow and hard. You can never imagine it, people dying from not having eaten for ten days, for twenty days. People recognize you only by your voice, your body is just a skeleton. People eat everything, everything: rats, crocodiles, snakes, banana trees, everything you can eat. With the communists it's terrible, it's terrible when they come to power. When they have their hands on everyone's stomach you can't do anything because you have nothing to eat. How could you even walk in the street like that? No, no. You don't have anything to eat. When you take a step it's already a huge effort and you risk falling over. The privileged class among the communists always have plenty to eat. They eat with everyone like the poor people in the villages, but when they return to their homes, they have chicken and everything else. It's terrible. The poorest person doesn't have any reason to revolt against them, because they are comrades."

"Since you know this, doesn't everyone else know this? They aren't naive are they?"

"They are very naive. That's sure, they are very naive."

"But not the people in the big cities."

"Yes, especially the people in the big cities. They are very naive because they don't know what communism is. They never lived one day with communism. Like you, for example, you don't know what is communism. You think, 'Oh, the communists are like us, they just have different ideas, that's all.' You are wrong."

"You have many interesting things to say."

"Uh no – it's that you've now understood what is communism, huh? You have to know what communism is. If you know the doctrine from books – oh that's completely false. In reality the communists are different – it's terrible." He liked to emphasize often with the phrase, *C'est terrible!*

"It's a kind of colonialism – a kind of totalitarianism very different from totalitarian regimes known in the history of the world – very different. This isn't the communism of Lenin, it's Stalinism, not communism. It's terrible. Millions killed in concentration camps, oh – it's terrible. You are from a rich country and you've known a democratic regime, the first thing you should think about is what?"

"Who, me?"

"Yes."

"You're asking me?"

"Yes."

"I didn't really understand the question."

"Umm, if you are wise, if you are intelligent, what do you do during your life beyond finding something to eat – what do you do?"

95

"What do I do?"

"I will ask directly. You'll understand easily. You have known a free life in a democratic world. You have known an easy and rich life in a rich country. That is to say, you have all you need to live easily. So, do you hope to continue this forever?"

"I hope so."

"*Voilà*. And not only for you but for your sons, for your grandsons, for a long time. You must think to keep by all means the democratic regime in your country and others too. That is, you are master of yourself, no one could dominate your country and install another regime. So you must make war against the communists since, if the communists conquered your country, they'd install a communist regime there. It would be too late, too late because they had already taken your stomach. And without that you can do nothing, nothing. So now is the time. Don't be too optimistic."

At this point I decided to get back to the reason I had come to see him.

"How many VC are there in your district?"

"Bien Hoa is the region where they have the most Viet Cong in the whole country. This region is the main entrance into Saigon, that's why this is the most important region from the point of view of information, of espionage."

"Where is your office?"

"Now in Saigon. There are lots of antennas on the building. There is a group of Chinese technicians who work for us to provide secret radio service."

"Chinese from China or Vietnam?"

"No, no. Real Chinese – imported to work for us. They have no contact with the outside world and after a few months we bring in a new team. It's on the third floor – no communication with the outside – it is very secret. There is no official designation, no signs at all."

"Do you interrogate VC prisoners?"

"That is done at the National Interrogation Center (NIC). If we uncover a VC we send him to the NIC. Our job is to have our agents penetrate into the camps of the Viet Cong. We receive information from the VC, not in our office but in their camps in the mountains. Our agents stay in the mountains and live there with the VC."

"Do you learn important information from these agents?"

"Yes. We knew, for example, in advance about the VC plans for Tet '68. We knew where they would attack – from what side. We alerted the government and then our function – our role – was finished. The Americans didn't believe us.

If for example we knew about the VC defenses, this information was conveyed to President Thieu but he didn't respond sufficiently."

"Do you know why?"

"Because the Viet Cong are very clever. They decided to make war in the villages. Many times; it wasn't the only time. That's why the other times they didn't follow through. It was a question of crying wolf; the Viet Cong started to attack or plan attacks many times but they always stopped before attacking. You know, it was like this in World War II. Do you know the film *The Man Who Never Existed*? There it was the same thing."

"Do you have female agents also?"

"Yes. Young girls. We have some everywhere. It's very difficult to send our agents into Viet Cong camps, you know – very difficult. To find someone dedicated enough to penetrate into the Viet Cong camps and live there and somehow get the information back to us. *C'est très difficile, très difficile.*"

"Have any of your agents been killed by the Viet Cong?"

"We take all precautions possible; not many, not many."

"How can your agents pass the information to your office?"

"There are resident agents and also liaison agents. The liaison agents have ways to recognize each other."

"Do they have rendez-vous in cafés?"

"No. Not in the cafés. In the foothills of the mountains in the jungle. The Viet Cong live in the jungle so the agents live there too with them."

"But I don't understand yet. If one of your agents infiltrates into the Viet Cong and lives with them, how does he give the information, how does he transmit that back to you? If the VC saw the agent entering your building, it would be finished for him. Does he telephone?"

"No. A police agent is dressed like an ordinary person and he goes to the house of a Viet Cong and looks for a friend of that family. He goes there as a friend. He meets also the Viet Cong relatives coming to see that family. If he learns something from the VC, he remembers it then he returns to the police department and makes his report. That's direct, that's very easy."

"Does he go personally to the office?"

"Yes, personally to the office."

"But if the Viet Cong saw him entering the building."

"For an agent who works in espionage, there are networks, you know; there are many networks. This agent reports to the chief of the network. Now a village chief, for example; everyone knows him as the village chief – but he has another function; that is to say, he commands this team, this network in that particular region, you know. And if the secret agents want to contact him, they don't come to his house, they go to a *maison de sécurité*, a safe house (he says it in English). In the forest, or in the town, or anywhere, a house that has nothing extraordinary about it from the outside but inside, it's different. So the agents meet in a safe house from where they send letters to places that we have already designated in advance. Afterwards, we meet through an intermediary; that is, our agent has an intermediary."

"Do the VC keep a list?"

"A dossier, a dossier. Of course. What they call a *liste noire*."

"Black list?"

"Yes."

"And we are surely on that list?"

"I think so," he says in English, laughing.

"I wanted to ask you again about counterespionage. Are you afraid of double agents; that is, Viet Cong who pose as government agents?"

"Yes, of course. You know, we sometimes use double agents. Our agents, even double agents, don't understand very much about what we are doing, and so don't have much interesting information to give to the other side. We always keep a great distance from the agents that we use."

"Couldn't double agents identify the real agents?"

"Yes, you're right. In the espionage service, if you don't work on a mission together, you don't know your comrade – never. It's only if you are on different missions. You have only the head of the network, the head of the mission, the chief, who knows all of the agents but the agents don't know each other. And we're sure that the head of the network is not a double agent. And then we have a man who follows and guards the chief; there are always two. That's why when the Americans gave instructions for that, they said, after we had finished the course, now we are no longer friends; if you meet me in the street I won't know you because you will be killed and I will be killed, too. If the enemy recognizes you, he will recognize me too since we are friends so we don't know each other. We never have conversations between agents unless it's urgent. These are the elementary rules in this field especially if one works in a foreign country. You have to take all possible precautions."

"We have been told to watch out for Vietnamese who don't seem to know their way around Saigon because they could be VC. One time I took a cyclo to my place on Tran Quy Cap and the driver didn't know the way, so I suspected he was a VC agent. Is that possible?"

"No, no, it's different. It's just the opposite. It's just the opposite."

"Why?"

"Well, your cyclo driver came from the countryside so he doesn't know the way. You know, there are many people who come in to Saigon from the country to work for a living. That's why Saigon grows to three or four million. But for a Viet Cong spy, you know, he never lets himself be noticed by people. He slips in unperceived, so no one pays any attention to him – that's the first thing. The second thing is that he tries to help everyone at every possible occasion, to gain the sympathy and confidence of the people. These agents are capable of anything from driving and repairing any kind of vehicle to taking a child to school; they can do anything. They can be a professor, they can speak English, they can translate; that is, they can do everything. They can penetrate everywhere."

"How many agents are there in Saigon?"

"Well, there are many but not people of that type, I mean experts like that."

"Do the agents carry weapons with them?"

"Yes, they have them but not on them. They bury them somewhere so that in case of emergency they could go get them, but not on them – it's too dangerous. They have personal weapons which they leave in the mountains behind a rock someplace."

"In our company villa we always wondered if one of our maids might also be a Viet Cong agent. Is that possible?"

"No, it's possible, but you know, the Viet Cong agents are in the bars."

"In the bars?" I felt my heart skip a beat as I thought about Thanh.

"*Ah, oui.* There are many in bars because of the military men when they are drinking, but unfortunately the soldiers don't know much. Maybe the officers know something – a battle maybe, but probably things just of local value only. Many of the bar girls work for the VC."

"Many?"

"Yes many, but they often get useless information – they are exploited. We have a secret service in the embassy – the 'Safety Division.' Access is difficult – it's difficult to get into this office. If you aren't in that department you can't enter."

"Do you have files on these agents – their names and descriptions?"

"Yes, of course we do. These files are very large and with all imaginable details."

"Would I be able to see them?"

"You take some tea?" he said, instead of replying to my request.

"Merci."

I continued with the interview.

"During the time of Diem, there was a lot of trouble because he was Catholic, wasn't there?"

"Ah, you know, Buddhism; we are Buddhists."

"You personally?"

"Yes. Buddhism is not a regime; no, it is a religion – disinterested. Buddha himself said, 'I am not a powerful man, I am not a god, I am nothing at all. But I am a man who knows before you, the deliverance,' that is to say reincarnation. After you die you would return as an animal, a man or a god depending on your conduct. So Buddha was a man who grants the deliverance. That's why we are free. We are free to be Buddhists, completely free. In belief there is liberty also. It's not like that with the Catholics. If you are Catholic, you must believe in God and Jesus Christ. But with us, it's different. I am Buddhist but I believe in Buddha because what he did and said interest me. I believe in what he said, but if you think that everything he said was not true then you wouldn't have to believe him. Buddha recommended, 'Do not believe in me if you know what I say is not true.' Yes, that's why in general the Buddhist religion is a completely free religion, completely disinterested. There is no pressure to be a Buddhist. President Diem had an older brother who was a Monseigneur – Archbishop – named Ngo Dinh Thuc. He administered all the Catholics in the center of Vietnam, you know. He wanted to rise up in the hierarchy of the Vatican – that's why he wanted everyone to become Catholic. He celebrated a big ceremony for himself to honor his rise in the Vatican's cardinal hierarchy. So all the Catholics raised the Catholic flag. It was also a holy day for the Buddhists – the birthday of Buddha – and we raised the Buddhist flag. The government had issued a decree that the National flag must fly in the middle of the religious flags. That day, the people in Hue raised the flags and the Catholics took them down. There was a dispute between the Catholics and Buddhists – just the religious believers. Afterwards, there was an incident and a Buddhist was killed by a grenade thrown by some village official. This created a panic. There was a protest demonstration by the monks in the streets of Saigon. Basically, I think, I'm not really sure, that the VC were always behind these things. They exploited the monks to protest against the government. We call this *Gia Dinh Chi*; that is, governing the country with the whole family – a government of the family (nepotism). It's not government by all the people. There is discrimination between Catholics and Buddhists. In reality Diem was Catholic but he didn't work for the Catholics. He didn't discriminate. I know this – I know personally because there were many bishops, many Catholic dignitaries whom Diem refused to receive."

"Did you know Diem personally?"

"Personally? Not personally."

"Did you talk to him?"

"Yes, yes, several times. Diem was a man who was very much a dignitary. He had a high opinion of himself."

"But didn't Diem order the attacks against the Buddhists?"

"No, no, no, no. These attacks – no one died because of these riots in the streets. Actually it was Nhu who was responsible for these riots. It was because Cabot Lodge was not happy with President Diem too, and President Kennedy was very far away from Vietnam – he didn't know. He knew only what Cabot Lodge told him and since Cabot Lodge was unhappy with Diem."

"Did you ever meet Cabot Lodge?"

"I met him one or two times. He's a man very like Diem; he possessed a great dignity of himself. His predecessor, (Frederick) Nolting, Ambassador Nolting, had real respect for President Diem. He was a very good man.

Diem said to Cabot Lodge, 'You wanted to be President – too bad.' That's why Cabot Lodge didn't like Diem. And then, the day that Diem was overthrown, President Kennedy was not in his office. There was just one presidential advisor there and he really detested Diem. Hilsman, I think, I don't remember (Roger Hilsman). He received the telegram from Cabot Lodge."

"What do you think was the turning point of the war so far, Tet '68 or the assassination of Diem?"

"No, the assassination of Diem. Tet was a defeat for the communists, a big defeat. If the Americans had dared to attack, they could have obtained any condition of peace. It was the fault of the press. You know the crimes the communists committed during Tet '68 in Hue, you know it's terrible. There were families buried alive, entire families. Buried alive. Barbarism. Terrible. Then the media said nothing about it. Really an injustice eh? Terrible."

"People always talk about My Lai and Calley."

"It's nothing compared to the crimes the communists committed in Hue. Buried alive entire families."

"I live in a little room next door to the family who owns a villa on Tran Quy Cap. When I moved in it was a special day for them and they were giving thanks by setting an altar with candlesticks, fruit and incense. Was that a Buddhist ritual?"

"I understand; it isn't Buddhist."

"It isn't Buddhist?"

"Yes, it isn't Buddhist. You know, all Chinese and Vietnamese, whether they are merchants or not, pay homage to the earth – to chance or Lady Luck. So this altar was for the goddess of Luck. This can be either in a corner of the house or outside on the ground. Yes, it's not Buddhist."

The Director's voice trailed off as he looked at his watch. The meeting was coming to an end.

As he stood up, he said in a hushed voice, "Let me know if there is anything I can do to help you in your report. We will work together as we discussed."

I was heartened by this statement and my hopes were confirmed – the interview had been a success.

CHAPTER 8

I stayed late at the office the next evening keypunching IBM cards to enter into the database on arrested students. I changed Minh's rating from A to C so that he could be released. I sent the program over to Data Processing. It always takes a day or overnight to run programs and get the output back.

The next day I received the output of my program and, as promised, sent the printout by courier to the director. How long would it take to get Minh released? And would there be trouble?

On my way home from work there was a tremendous traffic jam starting on Phan Dinh Phung, extending all the way to Hien Vung. I had to wheel the bike along the sidewalk. All traffic coming downtown on Duy Tan took up both lanes of the two-way street.

In the evening I went with some friends to town by taxi. As we entered the traffic circle by the old company villa, a Vietnamese policeman blew his whistle at us and signaled us to pull over. He approached the taxi and peered inside. Seeing me in the back seat he grinned broadly and said, "Oh, American – number one!" You never know what reaction you'll get by being American. There were lots of NPFFs (National Police Field Force) on Le Loi. War vets and students had rioted.

Wednesday, April 8
At the office today the manager told us they will hereafter report all those not at their desks by 0800. It's getting more "mickey-mouse" all the time.

The following note was passed around that VC snipers were supposed to be on Cong Ly and Cach Mang:

EXPEDITE!

Word has been passed down from J2 that there are VC all along Cach Mang and Cong Ly today. All civilian vehicles should BEWARE. Travel on the route as little as possible and LOOK OUT.

On my way home after work, when I got to the Caltex station I went through it and down to Cong Ly, keeping one eye open for snipers on the top of tall buildings.

Thursday, April 9

As we were filing in to a morning meeting in the CORDS Conference room, I quipped to Roger, "I guess I missed roll call this morning." "Yes, by three minutes," he said. So I said, "Why don't we get a time clock, then Roger can sleep late." Just then Brown comes around the corner and says emphatically, "We might - and then we'll pay by it!" He said it in his aggressive managerial style that irritated me. There was general dissention in the ranks about his ridiculous 0800 deadline.

I was anxious to hear back from the Director! At noon I wanted to take my mind off it so I hopped a cyclo to the *Blue Diamond* for an *omelette au fromage*. Their ad appeared in the local papers:

BLUE DIAMOND RESTAURANT – NIGHT CLUB

109-111 Tu-Do St. Saigon
PTT 20781
The Silver Bells and his Combo and Saigon's Favorite
Singers to Entertain with Miss Lien and ANNA
Excellent American and Chinese Dishes

After lunch I took a taxi to the black market shop, as I needed the cash. I was a little nervous so I looked first in a couple of other neighboring stores. Then I went in the shop. In the back the Indian men examined my two one hundred dollar bills closely. They looked up at me and said, "Why are they wet?" "It's from sweat riding the bike," I told them. For some reason that was OK and they went about the calculations for the deal. The rates were 410 for Piasters and 190 for MPC. I pocketed the bills and went out to the street, trying to look normal, and hailed a small taxi to MACV.

In the afternoon I bought a stuffed cobra and mongoose from the Thai store at MACV. I took it to my cubicle and put it on my desk. It would be a great conversation piece.

Everyone at HQ was talking about the rockets hitting Saigon last night. I had heard an explosion at 11:30 while reading in bed.

Wednesday, April 15
There were many reports in the local papers about the rocket attacks:

The Saigon Post:

RED ROCKETS SMASH INTO SAIGON ANEW

4 killed, 44 wounded
Saigon. Communist rocketeers zeroed in on downtown Saigon with four Soviet-built 122mm rockets Monday night.
Three of the dead and most of the wounded were in a theater. Another rocket struck the Ministry of the Interior (MOI). A third rocket landed in the Saigon River smashing windows in the Majestic Hotel. A fourth rocket landed in the tennis court at the plush Cercle Sportif, a country club favored by South Vietnam's political and social leaders and the diplomatic set. The series of blasts rocked the downtown area and sent residents scrambling for cover under furniture. Residents swarmed from homes and apartments and police cars and emergency vehicles darted back and forth along downtown thoroughfares, lights flashing and sirens screaming. Communist documents had indicated that another round of attacks was expected in South Vietnam later this month and an attack on Saigon itself might occur later this year.

In the morning I took a taxi to my Vietnamese female dentist. The driver was a bit surprised when I told him the address on Hong Thap Tu in Vietnamese.

She is quite disorganized for a medical person. No thorough inspection tooth by tooth or x-rays. She just fills the cavity where you say it hurts. One time I arrived, sat down in the chair and she said, "What was it we were going to do today?" This lousy Vietnamese water, according to her, is the cause of the bad teeth here. It doesn't have enough minerals in it, she says.

I walked back on Hong Thap Tu and stopped into a Chinese pharmacy with curious things in it, strange framed pictures of ancestors, Chinese characters on the wall, and all kinds of exotic-looking medicines, powders, etc. They weren't too friendly even when I spoke to them in French. They did ask me to sit down, maybe to try a potion or two? I demurred and said that I just wanted to look at the pictures, if that's possible. Similar reaction a little further on in a sundries store that had mirrors, toothpaste, notebooks, aluminum pots and pans hanging from the ceiling, and wine bottles with Chinese characters on the label.

Thursday, April 16

Last night at 2:30 I was woken up by rockets hitting again. I got that old tight feeling in the stomach – took a while to get back to sleep. Next morning on the 0700 news, right after the beep tone, the announcer said, "Rockets hit Saigon." He pronounced it like most Americans did, "SAI-gon" with the stress on the first syllable. They said three had hit, one on Hai Ba Trung at Phan Thanh Gian, one behind the USO (I thought of Paul), and one at Le Van Duyet at Nguyen Du (near Earl).

On my way to work today, I went up Hai Ba Trung to see what damage the rockets had done. Traffic was slowing down so people could get a good look. There was a big hole in the sidewalk and some bricks and roof tiles on the adjacent building were blown out. Otherwise, just some broken glass and rocks, but no big crater or wall knocked down like in a bomb blast. After the boom last night I could hear the ARVN artillery blasting away much louder than usual. The radio said they thought the rockets came from southeast of Saigon. Also a propeller plane could be heard making pass after pass over the area after the rockets had hit. I hope no rockets tonight.

Friday, April 17

The government was continuing to crack down on student anti-war protesters. According to the *Saigon Post*, the student demonstrations had begun with the arrest of Tran Van Minh, chairman of the Saigon Student Union. The government charged that Minh and other arrested students were members of a Viet Cong ring in Saigon. Lawyers for the students said that police had beaten and tortured a number of students, including a girl.

I needed to find out what the director had done. I had not heard back from him. Had he received the printout? Was there a problem? Was he telling the truth?

The next day I biked to work on time. No rockets last night but heard that a claymore exploded prematurely in a Lambretta in Cholon this morning. It was the first day of the new 1000 to 1200 office cleaning schedule. We always took advantage of this time to go into Saigon or out to lunch nearby at the airport. Miller posted a notice near the door requiring everyone to be back at 1300 "on the dot." I said, "I don't mind being back at 1300 or 1200, it's the 'on the dot' part that I object to." Others agreed.

There were reports from Cambodia about atrocities.

April 20 *The Saigon Post*:

SYSTEMATIC MURDER

SURVIVOR RECOUNTS CAMBODIA MASSACRE

DEATH TOLL OVER 1,000 PROBABLE

Phnom Penh "They started shooting at the men on the shore, first rapidly then slowly, as if going from one to another. My father was in the second group. They tied him up and made him get out of the boat. I knew what was happening to him and I knew what was going to happen to me."

The statement came Saturday from a 19-year-old Vietnamese who lived through a massacre by Cambodian troops of more than 600 Vietnamese civilians. The bodies wound up this week in the Mekong River.

Nixon announced today that he planned to withdraw 150,000 more troops in 1971, lowering the troop level to 284,000. "We finally have in sight the just peace we are seeking," he said. "We can say now with confidence; the South Vietnamese can develop the capability for their own defense."

In the paper last Saturday there was a photo of students squatting on Cuong De Street near the entrance to the Faculty of Letters of Saigon University where their planned third convention failed after police action. The photo showed armed, flak-jacketed soldiers standing over the students who were peacefully sitting on the ground. The soldiers carried rifles and shields against possible rock throwing by students.

Newsweek also carried news of the student protests.

The rain is beating down and it is pitch dark in Saigon. The broken mosaics on the sidewalks are wet and shiny and reflect strange shapes of buildings. A cyclo and its pedaling driver on the foggy mirror of a street are barely visible twenty feet away through the downpour. It is a clean rain and welcome in the oppressive heat. Always a relief even though one can get soaked.

Tonight I have a date with Nola, a tall American secretary at MACV. She works for a colonel. She was a bit stand-offish, but as Kipling said, "The colonel's lady and Judy O'Grady are sisters under their skins."

The other civilian guys are not attracted to American girls for the most part, especially the tall women they were escaping from in the US. Nola had given me the name of her apartment building, the "Central Palace," and the approximate location. I thought I knew about where it was but that evening in the inky black rainy city, nothing looked familiar. Every time I thought I was in the right place I was mistaken. I was going to be late and it would be the end of any possible romance that night – only anger. It was almost 9 o'clock when I finally got to the right apartment building and knocked on her door. Amazingly I was able to explain the delay and my apologies were accepted. I took it that she was as anxious as I was.

We went out to a nearby Italian place called Mario's for dinner. When we returned to her apartment, there was much drinking and smoking and the love making was simply a result of the drinking, nothing more.

The next evening we met again and went to the *Sportif* for a gin and tonic, then back to her place. We talked a long time, sipping our whiskies but she was cold as hell. Finally after one drink, she gives me that old speech, "I was drunk and I've hated myself ever since," and insists that I leave. Typical American female talk. I was becoming a believer of those who had come to Vietnam because they hated American girls. Did they espouse the East or renounce the West? This bit of romance was surely over and I was not disappointed.

As I was pedaling my bike home I could smell tear gas on Hong Thap Tu. I saw a Jeep full of QC with gas masks headed in the direction of the canal. There were also clouds of tear gas near the university on Cong De.

Next day at work I received a phone call from the Director of Police. Minh has been released! After work, at home, I took a quick shower, walked up to Flora's and told Thanh the news. She hung on me and beat her hands on my chest with delight.

CHAPTER 9

The head of the Saigon Student Union sent a telegram to US Senator William Fulbright informing him of the mass arrests and beatings of Saigon University students:

DEAR SENATOR FULBRIGHT:

A large number of students of the Saigon Student Union have been arrested for their protest against the war. The terms of their arrest are still unclear, as is their present whereabouts. They were apparently arrested for their criticism of the Thieu government. These students are in tremendous danger if something is not done soon to guarantee their safety. I cannot stress too much how important it is that you act quickly. These students have done a courageous thing. They are now suffering the consequences. Please act.

Sincerely,
(Signed) President
Saigon Student Union Association

In response, Fulbright sent a letter to Secretary of State William Rogers:

Hon. WILLIAM P. ROGERS,
Secretary of State,
Washington, D.C.

Dear Mr. Secretary: I am enclosing a copy of a letter and related material concerning the arrest of a number of student leaders in Saigon.

I would appreciate your having the appropriate officials of the Department (of State) investigate this incident as soon as possible and provide me with a report indicating what steps, if any, our government has taken or plans to take to assist the students involved.

Sincerely yours,

J. W. FULBRIGHT,

Chairman

Why was our government passing the buck in this important matter? Would our Secretary of State do anything about this? I doubt it. Loyal Vietnamese students were being arrested and tortured and our government was ignoring it. Why were we supporting this dictatorship of President Thieu? It made me really angry. I was determined to release as many of these students as I could.

In the meantime there was big news about an expansion of the war into Cambodia. On the front page of the *New York Times* was a photo of President Nixon pointing to the location of Cambodia on a large map.

I see more soldiers than usual in the streets, about six of them at the Ben Nghe Canal bridge that I cross on my way home from MACV. It is usually about seven p.m. when I pass the big pagoda on my right after the bridge. There is a huge bell outside the pagoda and sometimes, when the timing is right, I see a monk in saffron robe pulling on a rope attached to a heavy log, then letting go the rope so that the log swings back and strikes the bell, making a loud sound of a gong. This always gives me goose bumps as I ride by, a poignant feeling of being deep in the orient.

My bike now has no brakes left and I have to drag my feet to make it stop. I tried to fix the brakes at home after I had come back from dinner at the Splendid BOQ (Batchelor Officers' Quarters). The maid, as well as Monsieur and Madame, the owners of the villa where my room is, seemed glad to see me. They turned a light on for me and their little boy held a flashlight as I attempted to fix the bike. However, as I tried to tighten the brake cable, it snapped. The maid then offered to take it to the shop on Mac Dinh Chi the next day at six a.m. so that I could have it to go to work. I thanked her. I felt lucky that they were so friendly.

News is that the Paris peace talks are canceled for a week in protest against the US "invasion" of Cambodia. The total allied force now in Cambodia is 50,000, according to AFVN.

At work I joked with the guys that the COSVN headquarters they're looking for is really in tunnels underneath MACV HQ.

Student demonstrations were continuing.

May 6 *The Saigon Post*:

COPS NAB SQUATTING STUDENTS

The police early Tuesday morning moved against students occupying the former Cambodian Chancery on Le Van Duyet Street and took possession of the building. Between 60 and 70 were arrested and taken to police headquarters in police vans.

This caused a strong reaction. Students were up in arms when several were carted off to jail.

Tear gas has been a commonplace thing here and a couple of times I had gone through an invisible, acrid cloud of it on my bike. There were circumstances of "cowboys" throwing tear gas grenades while roaring down the street on their motorbikes. Actually the time I got the most tear gas was when I was headed downtown at night and saw a couple of jeeps full of Vietnamese policemen wearing gas masks speeding in the opposite direction toward Dakao.

About 1700, an urgent message was passed around the office at Headquarters that Saigon is off limits to the military for 24 hours and curfew is to begin at 2300; student unrest is given as the reason. Buddhists, students and veterans are said to be combining forces. Roger predicts a Big Minh coup overthrowing President Thieu within a week.

May 7 *The Saigon Post*:

Saigon, Gia Dinh Have New Curfew

New curfew hours will be observed in Saigon and Gia Dinh and will run from 11 p.m. till 5:30 a.m. effective Wednesday, according to an announcement by the office of the Saigon-Cholon-Gia Dinh military governor issued Wednesday morning. The previous curfew was from 1 AM to 5 AM.

The government, in a communiqué issued after a cabinet meeting Tuesday ordered all of the schools in the Saigon-Gia Dinh area, including Saigon University, to close Wednesday until further notice.

Prime Minister Tran Thien Khiem said Tuesday the government has to close the schools because the student struggle movement has assumed "a direction that may harm national security." He said some sections of the student population had managed to stage anti-war and peace-at-any-cost demonstrations and hinted the hand of "politicians and maybe Communists behind their actions."

It was a sweltering day at work with no air conditioning. The temperature must have been at least 100 degrees in the office. People left early on account of the heat.

I went to meet Ted at 8:30 in the *Green Light Bar* (Ly's bar) in Dakao. On the way, there was a cyclo driver who happened to be driving near me. I laughed with him and motioned that I wanted to race. He caught on and we both immediately accelerated. It must have been quite a sight, the two of us racing neck and neck in the "fast lane" of Dinh Tien Hoang. I could outpedal him on the getaway but he was more daring at intersections where I didn't trust Buddha – or my brakes – as much as he apparently did. We parted as I turned left onto Phan Thanh Gian, each laughing and shouting to the other, "Number One!"

As I walked down Mac Dinh Chi towards the bar in Dakao, I saw a group of Vietnamese soldiers at the corner of Phan Thanh Gian. They were watching a fire engine drive through the gates of the Mac Dinh Chi cemetery. What were they doing there? Before Tet '68, the VC had buried weapons and ammo in various Saigon cemeteries. Perhaps it was a bomb squad? In Saigon one was always left with these unanswered questions.

Ted was standing on the corner waiting for me. As I walked up to meet him a truckload of Vietnamese soldiers with rifles and mounted machine gun passed by. Also three rifle-carrying civilians walked past us headed towards Hai Ba Trung. Ted thought they looked like VC and that one carried an AK-47. Ted had heard the rumors too.

We settled at the bar and soon got to one of the usual topics of the time – the money black market. Ted said that the rate had been as high as 500 for green, but it was hard to establish a contact. Now it had dropped to 375, but he said they were all open for business again as usual. In the bars nowadays, the lights come back on already at 10:30 because of the new curfew.

Friday, May 8

I woke up tired, turned on the coffee, but decided not to go to work – not an easy decision as I was used to the routine of going to work every day. With the air conditioning at HQ probably still out of commission, it would be impossible to get much work done there.

I took a cyclo to the corner of Tu Do and Le Loi and walked to the "bookstore" to change money. The shop was of course a front. Inside there were glass showcases with small odds and ends, batteries, all manner of trinkets, cheap watches, etc. The actual money-changing counter was in the back of the shop behind a wood panel. Behind this counter was another secret room where the Indians undoubtedly stashed their money. While pretending to browse in the front of the store, you slowly wend your way in, glancing over your shoulder to see if the coast is clear before slipping out of view behind the panel. After a minute or two the Indian guys came out and I asked, "How is everything?" They laughed at this careful way of putting it. "No business now – too much trouble – maybe next week." They wouldn't even take green. So I slowly sauntered out, again pretending to look at the merchandise under the glass cases. At the same time as I was going out of the door onto the street a tall American came in. We both hesitated and looked at each other for a second. Before the door closed behind me, I heard him ask the Indians, "Do you have any soap?" "No soap," came the reply. A clever code I thought. And funny too.

In the evening I met a couple of guys from work and had a few beers at a local bar. Curfew was early and the situation in Saigon was precarious. Lots of soldiers in the streets and there are rumors of a coup on or about May 19 which is Ho Chi Minh's birthday.

And then there were more arrests of student anti-war protesters in Saigon. On May 11 the Stars and Stripes had the following shocking headline:

SIT-IN JAILS 76 STUDENTS

Apparently the police arrested 76 of the 2,000 students who were trying to occupy a government building in Saigon. They were protesting the recent detention of student leaders.

Next evening after work I went to Dakao, first checking out the downtown area to see what was going on there. Many soldiers were stationed along Cong Ly but nothing else was happening. Then on to Dakao and Flora's. Of course I wanted to find out if Thanh's brother was one of the students arrested. The little kids outside scrambled to "watch bike." They always got paid a few Piasters for this. I had a few Black Labels then Thanh appeared. We sat down together in a booth.

"Have you heard about the students arrested? Is your brother one of them?"

"No, he is not but he know many of them. Can you help them too now?"

"I will try."

"Will you buy me tea?" she said, and we both laughed. She was as usual very bright and cheerful and her smile made me feel good.

"I come over to see you if you want me to," she said, looking down in that mock modesty.

"Of course I do," I said, and took her hand in mine. She got up from the booth, cast a backwards smile at me and walked out the door. How many of these students did I dare to release? I ordered another beer.

When I left the bar, I went to buy a pack of Bastos cigarettes at the newsstand across from Flora's. I lifted up my bike from the street to the sidewalk to pick out what I wanted. The girl cashier noticed my cigarettes so I offered her one. She said, "You smoke Vietnamese cigarettes – too strong for girls."

On the way back home I was riding my bike, swerving for fun from side to side with no hands on the handlebars. A Vietnamese middle-aged man on his motor bike passed me, beaming a smile and said to me, "Very happy!" This really lifted up my spirits. Such riding is synonymous with being happy.

Tuesday, May 12

It's very hot these days, 95 and humid for the past two months. The monsoon season is giving us a preview, and one day last week I got drenched riding home on my bike in a sudden downpour.

Riding home from the Splendid, I had to stop with traffic at the circle by the cathedral to let Thieu's car and escort go by on their way to the Presidential Palace. The car was surrounded by four jeeps full of soldiers, police in front and back.

I was to meet Carl at Ly's bar in Dakao. At the gate on my way out of my room I met the maid and thanked her again for having the brakes fixed on my bicycle, but she wouldn't let me pay her for it. She said that it hadn't cost much. I thanked her for her generosity.

In the street there were soldiers with rifles lurking in the shadows – four or five of them. Funny feelings one gets walking past them knowing that they're looking you over, plenty of money – Western mercenary. This place is an armed camp these days, soldiers and riot police at almost every intersection.

At Ly's Bar, I talked to the Pakistani girl. "I wanted to talk to you but I was afraid to – you are so handsome," she said. "Sau" (liar), I replied, laughing. The French girl Hélène was wearing a new outfit and looked good. The fleshy, hippy girl was outstanding too, and broadly smiling as usual. The dancer, usually in a green dress, was in red top and black slacks. "Too Long," as I called her, was in her usual maroon jumpsuit. Several of the girls were wearing ao dais.

Soon Carl came in and joined me at the bar.

"There's an air of tenseness this evening," he said, after we had ordered our beers.

"Yeah, I can feel it too," I said.

Everyone could "feel" when there was this undefined tension – maybe it was the calm before the storm, maybe the presence of groups of soldiers, more than usual.

May 13 *The Saigon Post* headlined:

Red Rockets Slam Into Saigon Anew

SAIGON – Communist gunners fired rockets into Saigon early Tuesday in the first shelling on the capital since the allies launched campaigns into Red sanctuaries in Cambodia, military spokesmen said.

At least two and possibly three of the rockets, believed to be big Soviet-made 122 mm projectiles, slammed into the city of three million about 2 AM (1800 GMT), spokesmen said.

One struck in the section of the city near the presidential palace. Another struck near the Nationalist Chinese Embassy.

I was almost blasted out of my bed at night by the noise of the rockets. Three of them hit Saigon again, one in a field, one in the grounds of the Presidential Palace downtown, and one only two blocks away on Hai Ba Trung. I jumped out of bed into the bathroom to put another wall between me and the entrance where the blast would come from.

On the lighter side of life in Saigon:

The Saigon Post

TURKISH *Bath and* MASSAGE

Special steam bath house
A private bath rooms
By many beautiful girls, lovely and attractive to serve
Be courteous to the guests

117

> *Safety place*
> *A largest parking*
> *Located: 413-415 Phan-Thanh-Gian St. Sgn.*
> *Ticket: 400 piastre for each*
> *Open daily from 9.00 AM to10.30 P.M.*

> *Feeling Lonesome?*
> *Then come to Miss Gina's at 192*
> *Truong Minh Giang, Saigon (near bridge)*
> *We can solve all your problems adoption, companionship – marriage –*
> *villas and rooms for rent – cars many kind for hire. Cohabitation paper,*
> *driving licence, visa & passport extention of stay – Open 8 to 19:30 every day.*

After dinner with Earl at the Splendid I went back to my room. The owner knocked at my door and invited me to come over to the main part of the villa and have a beer with him. We talked about student and Buddhist unrest and the large number of soldiers in Saigon. He was worried about the situation as well. When I asked him his profession, he said he is a Mekong River pilot. What a title, I thought. He thinks that Thieu rules with the military too much, suppressing opposition.

Thursday, May 14

In the evening I walked down Mac Dinh Chi toward Phan Thanh Gian, which was crowded with cars and food stalls. Two shots rang out and I quickly ducked behind a nearby tree. When it was clear that there were no more shots I figured it was just the usual warning shots to stop some vehicle. Not far away at 95 Phan Thanh Gian, many people crowded around the open store front of a shop that sold ao dai's. Inside, about ten monks in saffron robes were standing in a circle bowing around an altar. One of them chanted the ceremonial funeral rites into a microphone connected to a big loudspeaker which boomed his voice into the evening streets. Suddenly, one of the shaven- headed monks, barefoot and wrapped in a saffron robe, left the shop and made his way through the little crowd toward me.

I was a little nervous, even though quite a few other onlookers had gathered around me also to listen and watch. I somehow felt that it was taboo for a westerner to view these secret oriental rites. The monk had one hand inside his robe. What was he clutching? I wondered. Then still another Buddhist came out and also walked directly toward me. I stepped aside to let him pass but he came right up to me and, in fairly good English, asked me if I would like to enter and witness the ceremony. I was uneasy about intruding and so declined politely, giving as reason the language barrier and that it would be difficult for me to understand. While we were standing at the edge of the street talking, I heard a couple more shots.

What a street, this, in Dakao; take a stroll to the neighborhood brothel, dodge some bullets and talk to a Buddhist monk at a funeral!

The monk explained that the family of the deceased call the monastery and arrange to have a group come and perform the ceremony. "We don't come unless we're called; we don't want to surprise anyone," one of them said. I had not expected such flippancy. A framed photograph of the deceased stood on top of the casket. "In the city," he explained, "the body only stays there for three days for sanitary reasons." As I left, we shook hands and the monk gave me a little "discourse" on friendship in English. He had memorized this little speech and gave a recitation staring fixedly straight ahead at my chest, spouting out the precepts while I listened attentively, looking down towards the small man.

The crowd around us was now quiet and out of the corner of my eye I could see everyone gaping at us, a very strange scene; a short, shaven-headed monk, barefoot, in yellow robes, reciting to an American, awkwardly towering over him. When the monk had finally finished, we exchanged names and he gave me the address of the monastery. He smiled, we shook hands and he said, "I look forward to seeing you again." "Yes, me too," I said.

I went to my room, got my bike and pedaled to Ly's Bar in Dakao. I had a cold beer and pondered over the events of the day.

Friday, May 15

Miller announces that there was a notice from J-2 (intelligence) that Buddhist riots are expected in the morning and names several pagodas, including the one on Cong Ly, and the An Quang Pagoda. Some discount this, especially Earl and Carl.

Sunday, May 17

I needed some instant coffee for my room so I went to the Central Market, looked around at the fascinating stands, found the coffee and bought a jar. At that point it seemed about to rain so I let that make up my mind for me and went, somewhat hesitatingly, to *Caruso's Bar*. Caruso's was one of my favorite bars because of a French girl named Jacqueline who tended bar there. Jacqueline asked, in her own restrained, blasé way where I'd been. We were going to go out but I hadn't felt like it.

As the electricity was temporarily out, there were candles on the tables and on the bar. This was producing more heat in the already hot day. As Jacqueline was busy with customers and couldn't talk with me, I left after two beers. Out in the streets, the acrid smell of tear gas hung heavy in the humid tropical air as I pedaled past the university on my way to Dakao to another bar.

At HQ a new MACV Directive was issued. It basically said that if you disagreed with the tactics used in the Phoenix program you were not obligated to follow them.

U.S. MILITARY ASSISTANCE COMMAND, Vietnam, DIRECTIVE NUMBER 525-36 - MILITARY OPERATIONS PHOENIX (PHUNG HOANG) OPERATIONS

Purpose. This directive establishes policy and responsibilities for all US personnel participating in, or supporting in any way, Phoenix (Phung Hoang) operations.

The Phoenix program is one of advice, support, and assistance to the Government of Vietnam (GVN) Phung Hoang Program, aimed at reducing the influence and effectiveness of the Viet Cong Infrastructure (VCI).

US personnel are under the same legal and moral constraints with respect to operations of a Phoenix character as they are with respect to regular military operations against enemy units in the field. Thus, they are specifically unauthorized to engage in assassinations or other violations of the rules of land warfare, but they are entitled to use such reasonable military force as is necessary to obtain the goals of rallying, capturing, or eliminating the VCI in the RVN. If an individual finds the police type activities of the Phoenix program repugnant to him, he can be reassigned from the program without prejudice.

X
Chief of Staff

This seemed clearly to be a way to cover their butts. I noted in particular the words:

"Unauthorized to engage in assassinations."

In my room I listened a bit to Radio Peking's propaganda broadcast.

Through the crackling static of the shortwave radio, the tinny but stirring revolutionary music wells over the air and a strong Chinese female voice announces proudly in French:

"Ici Radio Pékin." (This is Radio Peking). She plays a propaganda speech by *"Our great leader Mao Tse Tung"* repeatedly:

"People of the world unite to defeat the American aggressors and their lackeys! The Chinese people firmly support the three Indochinese peoples and all others around the world in the revolutionary struggle against the imperialism of America and its lackeys. American Imperialism seems like a colossus but it is in reality only a paper tiger. The Nixon administration is burdened by many difficulties, both domestic and foreign and the country is in complete chaos. The mass movement of protest against American aggression in Kampuchea (Cambodia) is having a chain reaction around the world. A small nation can defeat a big one if it stirs the masses — that is a law of history."

More student unrest was reported:

May 20 *The Saigon Post*:

Students, Police Tangle Anew At Buddhist Rites

Police lobbed tear gas grenades into a crowd of students and war veterans as they left An Quang pagoda, Cholon Tuesday morning.

A large number of students then retreated into the pagoda from where they stoned the police. According to the militants' leader, they are now declaring 'war' on the government – holding it alone responsible for the Buddhist charter of 1967 whereby the moderates are given preference.

In the afternoon I biked to Cholon. On the way I saw an old man on a bike with a little green wooden box on the back. On the box were the words, "HOT TOC" (barber). I thought I'd like to have it; I "coveted it," as Earl would say.

After dinner I rode down past the Hindu temple and noticed kids selling colorful posters on the temple steps. I walked my bike up on the sidewalk. There were dozens of kids. I bought three posters with huge, lurid pictures depicting wild scenes from Indian movies. One of them showed a bearded man in an embrace with his girlfriend. The kids asked 15P for each poster.

A little further on, a palm reader offered to tell my fortune. The palmist was somewhat older, perhaps old enough to remember some French. "*Combien?*" (How much) I asked. "*Cent* (100) *Piastres,*" replied the old man. He had a little layout right there on the sidewalk, some old paperback books on the orient, a large palmist's diagram of a hand, and a few candles. I reneged on the offer.

Back in my room Thanh was waiting for me! I had not expected this. She was excited like a puppy.

"Tomorrow you will meet my brother?" she said in a question that sounded more like a statement to me. "What?" I was completely taken aback by this.

"My brother will make speech tomorrow. A famous Vietnam patriot, Phan Khac Suu, has died and the students are planning a march – a protest march."

"Isn't that dangerous?" I said.

"I don't know, but he want to meet you."

"How can I?" I asked, "I don't know what he looks like." I was not sure I wanted to get in any deeper than I was already.

"But he know what *you* look like," she said. "I have told him."

"Are you coming too?" I asked with some anxiety.

"No, you must go alone," she said – just why I didn't know.

She then told me the location of the pho (soup) shop where her brother would be waiting for me.

"OK, I will talk to him."

"Oh, thank you," she said, and threw herself at me in a big hug.

CHAPTER 10

The local papers reported that student anti-war protesters would join the funeral procession tomorrow of a former Chief of State, Phan Khac Suu, who died Sunday.

Phan Khac Suu had been a loyal Vietnamese patriot and there were many headlines and obituary articles about him in the papers, including the *New York Times*. Suu had served as Chief of State in the first civilian government in 1964. He had been sentenced to eight years in solitary confinement for his part in an attempted coup, but was released three years later after President Diem was assassinated. He had also been sent by the French to the Poulo Condore camp, an island prison off the southern coast of Vietnam, for his political activities.

Friday, May 29

I was supposed to work today "if required," so I slept an hour late – to 8 o'clock, then decided to pedal downtown to change money before my meeting with Thanh's brother. Tu Do was blocked off below Le Thanh Ton so I turned right through unusually heavy traffic and locked my bike to a fence in the square by the City Hall Building. Student demonstrations had been predicted so I kept eyes and ears open as one learns to do quickly in Saigon anyway. Everything seemed OK at the Indian shop at 107 Tu Do. I thought this would be a good time to change money since everyone was busy watching preparations for the funeral. Rates were 375 for green and 185 for MPC. I talked to a GI on Tu Do who had only 9 days to go incountry. I told him he should watch the funeral but he said he didn't want to get involved so near the end of his stay.

As usual at this time of year, Saigon was very hot, but cloudy and hazy, threatening rain.

I found the pho shop easily and entered cautiously. I was the only non-Vietnamese there. One of the young men looked at me intently – this must be him, I thought. He approached me. He looked like a student, not from the lower working class.

"Hello," he said, smiling timidly and offering his hand. "I'm Minh, brother of Thanh."

I smiled too and we shook hands. I didn't mention my name. We sat at a table and he ordered some tea for us.

"You can help us," he said in a hopeful tone. "We are not communists, we are just students against this horrible war." His Vietnamese-accented English was fairly good. "We only protest war and we get arrested and sometimes even tortured."

"That is terrible," I said, the word seeming very weak. "In America they are protesting against the war also."

"Yes, I know," he said. "You know many students have been arrested. Can you help them too?"

"I will try to change their ratings as I did for you." I worried whether I would get away with freeing so many this time.

He said, "I thank you for getting me out of jail." Then he quietly laughed and said, "Vietnamese jails are not good place to be."

"I'm sure they are not," I said.

"You can give them aliases."

"Yes," I said, "I know how this works."

I knew that in Vietnam the family name comes first and the given name last. But there are relatively few family names, and so the given name is most often used for identification. Nguyen Van Thieu, the president of South Vietnam, is known by his given name Thieu, therefore "President Thieu."

Nicknames are universal and almost always reflect place in the family. A first son or daughter would be called Hai (Number Two); that is, second to the father. Second children are Ba (Number Three), and so on.

"Here are names of arrested students," he said, as he passed some notes into my hand under the table. His eyes flashed around continuously to see if we were being observed.

Frank Wadleigh

"We will be marching today in the procession," he said. "I am going to give a speech later at the cemetery if they let us in."

"I will do all I can," I said. He smiled and said, "Good, we all thank you."

We parted separately. I went back to watch the funeral procession and tried to locate Minh and the students in the crowd.

As I looked up the street, I could see the procession stretching all the way to the twin-spired cathedral, just visible behind the tall trees. It was moving slowly down towards the Continental Palace. The name CONTINENTAL PALACE in large letters on a white, clapboard sign stretches along Tu Do and continues around the corner on the side facing the National Assembly building. Bamboo awnings hang down from this sign, to keep out the sun and monsoon rains. Large potted palms stand at regular intervals along the sidewalk where people used to sit at tables in the old days until it became too dangerous on account of VC grenades. In most of the second floor windows of the hotel are air conditioning units, but today the windows are open and their lace curtains swing idly in the slight breeze. The street is packed with onlookers: businessmen in white, out-of-trouser short-sleeve shirt, only rarely with tie, groups of small children, attractive girls in ao dais, some holding parasols. In the shade of awnings from the floor above are the many shop fronts with signs in Vietnamese, English, and French. There are Chinese men in their typical garb of trousers and sleeveless undershirt, and a few women carrying babies. Those men in dark suits and shades look like security police.

Some onlookers shove their way through the crowds on the sidewalks into the street itself. Vietnamese paratroopers in camouflage uniforms, red berets, and white gloves hold their rifles while standing at parade rest. Many VIPs are on the steps of the National Assembly building. Lam Son Square is always the focus of attention for foreign news cameramen. Today there are also military cameramen standing in an army deuce-and-a-half truck.

Leading the procession and first to enter the square is a military jeep creeping along, a Quan Canh in dress whites standing inside, bracing himself with one hand on the windshield of the open vehicle as he looks back at the long procession behind him.

Everywhere there are large, white banners proclaiming Suu as a valiant revolutionary. People are leaning out of the windows in the Caravelle Hotel. A large sign on the front of the hotel says "Air France."

The first deuce and a halfs are beginning to arrive, their windshields flipped up to catch some breeze. They are bedecked with black, purple, and white ceremonial palls with Vietnamese and Chinese writings. The large crowd has now turned its attention to the arriving procession.

It seems strange that a funeral for a civilian would have these huge military deuce-and-a-half trucks at the head of the procession. They are indeed incongruously bulky and high with their exhaust pipes sticking irreverently in the air. One truck is draped up to its headlights and grill in white and black palls with dragons and circular patterns of Chinese characters.

Next comes a civilian band of drummers and flutists, played by men in shirtsleeves and tie. Behind them is a float with a large vertical, multi-colored banner, mainly saffron, with Chinese writing in round patterns and a pink curtain over the edges. Further up Tu Do is a multi-storied hotel with people looking out from balconies.

A man in pith helmet holds the reins of a horse-drawn cart bearing an elaborate float. The two horses have yellow ribbons tied to their ears. Another man stands on the float tapping a large red and black drum. Branches of fruit trees wind up an altar with brass candlesticks. On this float is a large altar with bowls of fruit stacked on mahogany pedestals forming wooden demons. Incense smoke winds its way between brass candlesticks. This is followed by another musical group dressed in white.

A huge 'dragon' is now visible up the street, on which sits the catafalque bearing the coffin. The dragon is preceded by a group of a dozen men in black whose job is to pull the motor-less dragon with ropes. Motorcycle policemen drive slowly alongside. The long neck of the dragon protrudes out in front, ending in the figurehead of a ship, a frightening Chinese monster, mouth open, teeth bared, and piercing eyes. On the back of the dragon, like the shell of a snail, is the catafalque itself consisting of an ornamental tent representing the dragon's body covering the coffin which is barely visible through an opening in the square "body" of the dragon. The tail protrudes far out in the back. People, possibly relatives of the deceased, wearing white headbands sit on the dragon float between the catafalque and the dragon head. One young girl among them cools herself with a pink hand-held fan.

The dragon float has now finally entered Lam Son Square. Mourners follow the catafalque, many holding pink or white parasols over their heads against the hot sun. The entire square is now bulging with people, floats, banners, parasol umbrellas, groups of musicians, military bands, film cameramen, and the air resonates with cacophonic music of drums, cymbals and various wood instruments.

The funeral cortege is accompanied by marchers from various opposition groups, including close to five thousand students. With their pennants and banderoles flying they move along the street chanting "Down with the militarists!" "Down with corruption!" In front of the presidential palace they had forced the procession to stop for a few minutes and shouted out their slogans.

The goal of the procession is the Mac Dinh Chi Cemetery, a few blocks away. Once arrived at the cemetery the huge crowd of unruly students is prevented from entering. When President Thieu, Vice President Ky, and a small group of government dignitaries had finished their speeches, a small representative group of students were allowed in.

The obvious leader of the students was then permitted to speak. I could see it was Minh himself. He started to speak in a quiet tone but as his speech continued, he became more and more aggressive and agitated, accusing the government of having betrayed Suu while he was alive, and now burying him in the Mac Dinh Chi cemetery where many French colonialists had been buried. He shouted that the students would take revenge. Then the group of students forced their way out of the cemetery, saved from arrest, I assumed, by the presence of many foreign news reporters.

The next day all the papers, including the *New York Times*, reported the funeral in headlines:

PHAN KHAC SUU, 65, SAIGON OFFICIAL
President of the Constituent Assembly in 1966-67 Dies

That evening at HQ, I changed the classifications of the students that Minh had given me and sent the document to the director by courier as usual. This would be a big step, changing the files on so many students. Would the director agree to this? I was beginning to worry that I was getting in over my head and that this would certainly arouse suspicions. Still I felt that I could not let these brave young students suffer in jail and possibly be tortured.

Next day at work life returned to normal with the usual numbers game, more data, more analysis and more paper shuffling.

At lunch I went to look at the Thai souvenir shop where there was a cute Vietnamese gal we nicknamed "The Snake Lady" because she had sold me the stuffed cobra and mongoose that I have on my desk. She asked me in Vietnamese, "Where's my card?" I had promised to send her a card that she liked. I asked her to write down her address and said I'd send it to her. She did not want to do this. I told Earl about this later and he said that many Vietnamese do not want to be known for corresponding with Americans. He said he would talk to the Snake Lady, then told me how I should address and word the card to be sure it would not appear to come from an American. He wrote me a note:

Do not, under penalty of excommunication, put your name or anything else on card or envelope that will identify the sender as an American. TYPE or have written by a Vietnamese.

12:00 news: fighting in Dalat. Sounds bad. It's only a matter of time before Saigon gets it too. I took all breakable stuff off the top shelf and put it out of the way. We may get rockets tonight. Who knows?

The rainy season has arrived. After each rain the air smells good and clean and the sunsets are beautiful. In the evening after dinner it's cooler and I bicycle down to the waterfront of the Saigon River to look at the freighters and navy ships. The lights at night transform everything into a sort of calm oriental mysticism. The contrast of old French red-tiled roofed buildings and little Vietnamese carts selling all kinds of weird concoctions is striking. At night there are many of these carts on wheels displaying dried fish hanging in rows. Some carts sell sandwiches made with big loaves of French baguettes.

Thursday, June 4

After work I cycled home, then went to the movie at the *Institut Français*. Just as I was locking my bicycle to the iron fence in front, a girl gets out of a car, saying "Merci," to the driver. I let her go first up to the ticket window. She didn't know that the price was 100P this time. With presence of mind completely lacking, I failed to pick up the tab before she had to search in her wallet. I sat two seats away from her. She seemed entranced by Chateaubriand's *Mémoires d'Outre-Tombe*, spoken by the French actor Pierre Fresnay, and she laughed happily throughout the film *Les Quatre Cents Coups*. The end of the film came abruptly. The boy in the movie escaped from the juvenile delinquent home and walked toward the ocean. Then blip – his face is big on the screen and the movie ends. The lights go on and everyone files out. The girl was nowhere to be seen. I thought she probably had been picked up by someone in a car and whisked away. Then as I rode down Le Thanh Ton, almost at Hai Ba Trung, there she was in a cyclo. I smiled at her but she was too far away. I felt that it was too bad I hadn't said something.

I felt a warmness, an electric feeling but had been too cautious, too withdrawn and introverted that evening. I was mentally prepared for a movie only. There's always the hope that she'll be there next week. That never seems to happen but I'll probably go anyway. There are many reasons for not bothering. Why get involved? Yet she was *sympathique*, as the French say.

Back in my room. It's 11:30 and there's the sound of rain on the tin roof. Both ceiling fans are on as usual. I ponder over what might have been.

CHAPTER 11

The papers announced the release of most of the students! The director had not failed me.

The Saigon Post:

73 Students Freed; 3 Will Stand Trial

The Saigon court Monday released 73 of 76 students who were arrested recently in front of the Ministry of Education where their attempt to hold a demonstration was foiled by police.

The remaining three students, all leaders of the Saigon Students Union will be tried by a military court, according to the court's ruling. They will answer charges of having organized demonstrations in defiance of an order late last week of the Saigon - Gia Dinh Military Governor's Office.

The court's decision touched off an uproar from among some 1,000 students who gathered inside and around the court premises which was sealed off with barbed wire and guarded by riot police. But they were dispersed later by police who lobbed tear gas grenades into the crowd and chased them out of the place down to nearby streets in downtown Saigon.

I went to Flora's to see Thanh and tell her about meeting her brother. She was so happy about the students freed and asked me about the other three. I said I would try to free them as well but the situation was getting very dangerous. That evening I sent the names of the three students, with their changed classification, again to the director. It may be more difficult to free them than the others.

Thursday, June 11

In the evening I walked over to the *Institut Français* but the girl from last week wasn't there. In the movie *Mouchette*, a school girl who refused to sing in the chorus with classmates was punished by the teacher who pushed her head down against the piano keys while she, the teacher, banged out the tunes. "I play the tunes and you are to sing." It's like working for someone – they play the tunes and you'd better sing or else. Horrible. The girl in the film reacted by throwing mud at her schoolmates, then running away and hiding. It seemed symbolic that they never tried to retaliate – almost as though they were in different worlds.

Walking back from the cinema, it started to rain hard and I had to find shelter under the overhang of a building on Hai Ba Trung. Across the flooding street, rain angled against the grey stonework of an ugly, monolithic, barracks-like building reminding me of similar, cheerless structures in East Berlin. As I stood there watching the pouring rain, I could hear the distant thumps of "outgoing." They had different pitches – sometimes a low, muffled boom, other times a quick one-two of higher-pitched, smaller pop-pops.

On my mind these days was the thought that one seems to lose something in Saigon as day in, day out, one tries to act like a machine, getting up early enough, being on time, going through all the motions. Lunch every day in the cafeteria with hundreds of soldiers, gulping down the food, reading old news, looking in the PX for something new, then returning to the desk where one sits until six o'clock. By the time dinner is over it's 8:00 in the evening. But pedaling around the side streets of Saigon after dinner in the cool of the evening and absorbing the sights, sounds and smells is fascinating and keeps me going.

July 1 *The Saigon Post*:

US Pullout from Cambodia Completed

SAIGON – About 1,700 American troops, most of them slogging on foot through monsoon mud, crossed into South Vietnam Monday to end a two-month US campaign against Communist sanctuaries in Cambodia, military sources said.

Tuesday, July 7

It rained hard this morning as I was ready to leave for work. I would have been late anyway so when it let up, I decided to take advantage and biked down to Tu Do to change money. Outside the shop I cautiously looked around as the Indians were standing out in front. I locked my bike to one of those metal telephone girders, sauntered up the street, trying to look like a browsing shopper, even to actually entering the stamp, coin, and antique store next door. The old lady there opened the glass case so I could see the stamps, but she couldn't have known I was more concerned about two Americans I had spotted on the second-floor balcony across the street. I had already checked them out, using the storefront glass as a mirror. Were they spying, seeing if I used the black market? Finally I left and wandered into the Indian "novelty" store. I mumbled "How's everything?" While they counted out the bills one of them told me to go away from the back and be "shopping, you know." Once I had the wad of Piasters and MPC I was glad to finally get out of there. This time the rate was 190 MPC to the dollar and 375P to the dollar.

Wednesday, July 8

After dinner I rode down to the Central Market to look around. There were women in the street stringing colorful necklaces made from little "pastas." I thought it would be fun and crazy to wear a couple of these when I went to Jacqueline's. I bought a little pocket flashlight and one of those typical pith helmets cyclo drivers wear. I felt in a nutty mood and pedaled to Caruso's wearing the pith helmet and pasta necklaces, lighting my way with the little flashlight. At Caruso's Jacqueline and I laughed at my outfit. I had a couple of lemonades as I was thirsty. We joked around a lot and I blurted out with, "Will you go to bed with me?" "Yes," she said, grinning. She had to wait on a customer and said, "Just a minute, I'll be right back and we will." I said, "You're chicken." She insisted she wanted to and said, "You wouldn't believe your ears if you knew how much." But it was subject to the condition that I come back and go upstairs where her husband Michel was. She was always putting that condition on – that it had to be a *ménage à trois*.

I left about 9 to meet Earl at the *Green Light Bar* – aptly named, for anything goes there and usually does. The girls will suddenly, in a playful mood, grab you in the privates! I mentioned to Earl that it seemed to me that Vietnamese girls aren't satisfied with the shapes of their noses, which are usually pug. They clearly prefer Western ones. Earl said, "That's really true."

The Saigon Post reported:

Reds Shell Hue; Hospital Hit, Two Killed

US Forces Here Down To 417,100

Students Announce New 'Struggle' Move

The Saigon Students Union is prepared to launch what its leaders called "a new phase of struggles" despite recent warnings by President Thieu that the armed forces might be called in to suppress further students unrest.

Saigon Peace March. Saigon police used tear gas to break up a peace march of about 1,000 South Vietnamese college and high school students and a small group of visiting American pacifists. The Vietnamese demonstrators were marching to the National Palace to deliver a statement demanding an end to the war and the Americans were en route to the US embassy to submit a similar petition. Both groups joined for part of the way and police disrupted the procession.

About 30 students and three American correspondents, wearing black peace armbands, were arrested. All were later released. The newsmen included John Steinbeck IV, son of the late author and part-time correspondent for CBS.

It was good that the students were getting more international concern.

The next day I was happy to see the headlines in *The Saigon Post*:

Court Frees 3 Students

The prosecution office of the Saigon Court of First Instance Wednesday released three detained student leaders. They were among the 76 students arrested for defying a government order banning demonstrations. The others were freed by the court.

The case of the three was forwarded by the Court of First Instance to a military court on the ground of lack of jurisdiction but the latter also refused to try them.

I rode to the Splendid for dinner, then afterwards to Thanh's bar. She was pacing back and forth looking down at the ground. When I arrived, she burst into enthusiasm, coming close as though she wanted to kiss and hug me but is too timid. "I wait for you so long. I think you never come." She was overjoyed about the three students.

Next day I met Earl at the Splendid and after dinner rode with him on his Honda to the *Golden Dragon Bar* on Cong Ly but it was dead so then to a bar on Nguyen Hue that has a couple of young French girls. We first sit at the bar but the cockroaches crawling along the bar drove us to a table. I bought a 400P tea for one of the girls. A girl Earl had known before came over and sat with us. He told me of her possessiveness in buying a sweater with his money at the "I House" (International House). The French gals, who were "cherry" according to Lien were in bare midriff, green pants and tops. "Mine" was in a green dress.

Saturday, July 18

They said that two rockets crashed into Saigon at about 3:30 in the morning but I hadn't heard anything. Only one, it was said, had exploded on Cong Ly near the Palace. It was in the paper. Explosions reverberated throughout the downtown area.

No rain today. Temperatures average in mid-90's these days, as it has for a long time.

Miller came up to my desk holding my time card and asked about the two days I had come in late. I explained that I had been staying late. Miller said also that Brown was going to announce the requirement that everyone has to wear a tie. "Oh," I said, in sarcastic excitement, "We're all going to get promoted." He gave me a dirty look.

Earl and I talked with the girls in the Thai shop at MACV. One of them had jokingly accused me of calling her old and ugly. They have a penchant for making up outright fabrications if they have nothing else to talk about. Cases in point: nutty Miss Ly of Dakao and her accusation that I had stopped up the bar's toilet with paper leaflets proclaiming "Saigon Tea Fini." Also the maids at the old villa had accused me of making my Vietnamese language tutoress pregnant.

Thursday, July 23

Still no rain today. Clear blue skies – only a few clouds. Hot. Dave and I walked over to Tan Son Nhut for lunch. I had a chicken and ham sandwich and Dave a steak sandwich. We watched a Pan Am flight land with passengers, mostly Americans from the "real world." How strange they looked.

They had attaché cases in the PX today. I bought one for a Vietnamese lieutenant as the Vietnamese are not allowed in the PX.

In the evening I rode over to Dakao to Kim's bar. On the way I saw Thanh. Even though it was dark and difficult to see I recognized her walking with that straight proud bearing. Her long, black hair hung over her ao dai. Her well-rounded hips swung from side to side. She wore a string of jasmine around her neck. She was surprised to see me. We hugged briefly and I said I could give her a ride home.

She sat side-saddle on the back of my bike and we crossed that crazy bridge which is really two bridges, the one on the left more solid, concrete, with asphalt top. The one on the right entirely of wood slats laid cross-wise. After I left Thanh in front of her place and headed back towards Dakao, I got lost and ended up somehow in the entrails of an ARVN compound and their clutter of shack-like family dwellings – more "oriental" than the rest of Saigon. There was an old car parked there, a black, skinny Ford "Popular," or so it said on the hood ornament.

Friday, July 24

After the military bugle sounded retreat, there was a very brief rain as I pedaled towards the Continental Palace where I was to meet Earl at 8:00. We ordered drinks but one of the incessant beggars that hang around the Continental Palace kept pestering us, reaching up from below at the sidewalk level with dirty outstretched hand. We decided to have dinner at *La Cave* on Le Loi St.

After dinner I went to my room, showered and walked up to Flora's. Just had one beer. Tired as usual. Thanh thought I looked sad. "I always look sad," I said. Thanh said, "I try to look happy but inside I really break." She said if I didn't want to talk to her I didn't have to. Later she mumbled, "What if I said I might want a drink?" I didn't answer her. As I left she was sitting in the corner by the door. I saluted goodbye but she just looked sad and dejected and made no sign at all. I went home by Honda.

Saturday, July 25
Our manager Brown held a big meeting at 0900. "Contract has been signed but money is very tight," he warned. No $400 Cost of Living Allowance. MAC flights available but only to Hawaii or the West Coast. "Competitors are barking at the door." At least I still had a job.

Sunday, July 26
In the evening at Caruso's, Jacqueline said she's going to Nha Trang in a week or two. Will stay there for a couple of months or however long it takes her to get tired of it. She's done this several times in the past, when she got "nervous" and wanted to be "free." She always comes back though like a spoiled child. Towards the end of the evening she said to me, "You are very quiet, very calm," and that I should keep that, but that I was "too good" for her. This latter comment was to bother me much more afterwards as my mind replayed the 'tape' of the conversation again and again. The full force of people's remarks never seems to have full impact until much later, usually long after anything can be done about it except to dwell on it.

Monday, July 27
George, one of the CORDS' analysts, came back from vacation today and moved into the desk opposite mine. He had worked in the Annex and so I had never met him. I was relatively quiet all day and at the end of the day he said, "You are quieter than I had been led to believe."

I said, "I'm sorry to disappoint you."

"It wasn't a value judgment – just a statement of fact," he said, grinning in a sort of friendly way. I just smiled back, a bit puzzled – who had told him I wasn't quiet?

Ted was out today. He had made the mistake of passing a personal check to the Indians' money black market shop on Tu Do to get Piasters. The authorities had raided the shop and turned one of his checks over to our company. This could mean that he would be thrown out of the country. He phoned me and wanted to meet at Flora's at 9. It was Thanh's night off so we just drank and I told him it was too bad he wrote a check. I did tell him that it was a pretty dumb thing to do. He told me the story of his cheating girl friend. He somehow remained stoic about everything and kept that ironic smile on his face.

Wednesday, July 29

Met Earl at the Splendid for dinner. We went to Flora's and joked about the new 'tie rule' at Headquarters and wild kinds of them we could invent to ridicule this stupid idea. He told me about George's see-through one made of plastic overlay material. He could write on the acetate the color of the "tie" and later in the day write on it with a black crayon, "This is a white tie." We joked about wearing a long tie as a combo tie/loin cloth or codpiece. This provided a lot of laughs.

After dinner at the Splendid I watched the movie and, while they were changing reels, I looked in on the TV room. A girl was giving the weather report in the States, temperatures around the country, 87 degrees in Dallas "today," but no one here knows what "today" is. Let's see, there's 15 hours' difference to the west coast and it's Sunday, about 8:00. That makes it last night. They must mean the temperature yesterday. The time thing boggles your mind here; it's a big bubble of uncertainty. Does anyone really know what time it is?

Saturday, August 8

Every day I look out the window at the office and wish I could be outdoors.

Late that evening George and I tried to get one last beer on Hai Ba Trung, but they said, "Too late." On leaving me off at my place, he said something like "I guess I'll see you Monday." I said, "Yeah, they can't fire me on Sunday, can they?" He moaned, "Oh, good night," and off he went on his bike. Not unfriendly but for me sort of abrupt. That's his style though.

Sunday, August 9

I rode to the Central Market and down Ham Nghi to the river to see if any interesting big ships were in port. It didn't look like it so I went back, thinking I'd go to Cholon – maybe I could even find the maker of those small, wooden wine pitchers that they had at Ramuntcho's. I rode along Nguyen Cong Tru ("win come true"), a highly oriental-looking street, becoming more and more Chinese with real rice-roots markets, apothecary shops and printing presses for Chinese newspapers. Coolies in undershirts scurried around in the heat and humidity. It suddenly became very cloudy and looked like rain so I headed back toward Saigon. On the street taking me back to Nguyen Cong Tru, I noticed a store full of colorful incense and other fascinating orientalia. I doubled back, pulled my bike up on the kickstand and slowly started to enter. Everyone inside the darkened interior of the shop stared at me, curious about what I wanted there. They had all kinds of Buddhist colored votive paper, incense sticks, a million types of tea, bamboo pens, writing paper, and lots of colorful signs in Chinese characters. I ended up buying two boxes of incense, three bamboo pens and ink for calligraphy. It started to rain and a strong wind blew down tree branches onto the street. I managed to get home without becoming totally soaked.

Monday, August 10

Tough day. Have to finish a technical report on HES. Carl had written me a note in red ink that he wanted it "By COB today." Those initials meant "Close of Business." Sometimes in true military acronym fashion they wrote "NLT COB," or "No Later Than Close Of Business," followed by the day or date that it was due. I worked till 8:15, then George and I went to the Mass. It rained like mad just as we got ready to leave. We ran out the doors of MACV to the military bus. A wire had blown down across the path of the bus and the driver jammed on the brakes to avoid hitting it. Was it live? There were lightning flashes and tremendous thunder. Rain was pouring over the windows of the bus and the wind blew the rain in. Some GIs with rifles and full gear piled out of an APC (Armored Personnel Carrier) and into the bus. Some were cursing the rain. At the Mass all the lights were out except upstairs. By the time we had finished a beer and something to eat, the rain had stopped and we rode the Honda to a bar on

Cach Mang. There was a girl in red dress sitting at the bar. George pointed out that on first sight it looked like she had a tremendous girth.

Tuesday, August 11

In spite of my hangover I managed to get up and catch a taxi to work. I wanted to finish the report that was supposed to have been done by COB yesterday. I was at my desk writing by the time Carl walked in. "The infamous Conditional Probability Sensitivity report," I said, as Carl nosily looked at it. He showed no reaction, adding to my annoyance.

In the evening I rode my bike to meet George at the Splendid. It was threatening rain. As George passed me on his Honda I yelled "We're not going to make it." And we didn't. The rain came down in buckets. George pulled over as did most of the others on bikes and Hondas. I went on anyway, yelling "See you there."

After dinner I rode the bike home and then went with George on his Honda looking for a good bar. We went again to that bar near Caruso's where there were those two crazy girls. On the way out the one in red dress was standing in the doorway. I asked her, teasing, "You come home with me now?" "Have to work," she said, laughing. "You come back at 11 o'clock OK?" "OK," I said.

Wednesday, August 12

At my room there was a note that Earl had left for me. It was written on a piece of old company notepaper.

8: 15 PM
12 VIII 70

Stopped by – hadn't seen you at the Splendid for several days running. Maybe there's been a flap at MACV. Will try to call you tomorrow – Earl.

Earl always wrote the month in Roman numerals to avoid ambiguity between day and month.

Friday, August 14

There was a new rule at the office that everyone had to sign out whenever they left. Another "Mickey Mouse" rule we all agreed. They had put a sign-out board near the door. So when George and I went out to the snack bar for a coffee we wrote in protest:

OUT: *9:32*
RETURN: *9:47.*

When we got back Miller balled us out, and said this was "An affront to authority." This whole sign-out rule was disgusting and we got a deserved laugh at it.

Saturday, August 15

There was a going away party for a major at the restaurant called "Seven Kinds of Beef." After the party I went with George bar hopping. First we checked into Flora's and Thanh said she was going to Can Tho. I tried to convince her to get out of the bar business but she said she has to "repay" her parents.

George and I got pretty drunk at a bar on Cach Mang where we met a French gal. I asked if I could take her home. "No, I never do," she said.

Sunday, August 16

I woke up at about 9 with another headache. A few minutes later the bell at the gate rang. It seems the people here don't answer unless they're expecting someone. I went to the gate and it was Thanh. We went to my room and she showed me some calligraphy with a pen I bought in Cholon. Burned some incense and she stayed the night.

Monday, August 17

Radio says the entire Pacific B-52 fleet are hitting northern I ('eye') Corps. Pounding of artillery can be heard almost nightly here.

Tuesday, August 18

It was still raining in the morning so on with the overnight-dried raincoat and onto the bicycle to work. By the time I was nearing Tan Son

Nhut I was getting hot and sweaty and wished I had just put the raincoat on the back of the bike. Shoes take a beating – splattered with mud. Proofed some HES reports and submitted computer runs for Non-Hamlet Population. Cooler these days, 85-90 daytime.

In the evening Thanh and Lien were waiting by my gate. They were all excited, bouncing up and down. They wanted me to get Ong Hung (their name for Earl) and come talk to them at their new place of work, the *Lotus Bar* at 142 Tu Do. I said "OK I will." In my room there was a note that the maid had left. It was a message that Thanh had conveyed to the maid and said:

Miss Thanh wants to see you at 142 Tu Do.

I pedaled over to Earl's house but he wasn't there so I wrote him a note on the one I had received from him. Then I rode to Tu Do in a light rain, many puddles and slick, black, shiny streets. At 142 Tu Do a little girl about 9 or 10 years old was standing out front selling jasmine. As I locked my bike to the grill gate of the shop next door, she looks at the bike and says, "Why you go like this, why you don't go Honda?" I say, "No money."

I went inside. They were happy to see me, but it was a typical bar so it was not clear why they were so excited about it. It was hard to understand their way of thinking.

Wednesday, August 19

Rain started again at 5:30 p.m. George asks me where I'm going to eat. We decide to go to the Mass BOQ for dinner and then to a bar with "Hawaiian" girls. George gets annoyed at 150P beers. To Lotus bar. Thanh has the night off but Miss Lien is there. She talks in a crackling voice as usual.

Today is the 29th anniversary of the Viet-Minh. The numbers of police and soldiers have increased. An appearance of glassy quiet has settled over this capital, which has been agitated for months by demonstrating students, Buddhists, and veterans. The rainy season continues and I continue to get wet and mud-splattered on my bicycle. The rain usually waits until about 6 or 7 when I am leaving work on the bike. The rest of the day is usually sunny and warm, if not hot.

Friday, August 28

Up at 6:45 as usual. Make coffee. Bike to MACV. But hundreds of Hondas, bicycles, and enormous crowds of people are gathered outside the gate. I recalled hearing that Vice President Agnew was supposed to arrive today. I thought I could maneuver around the crowd but Vietnamese cops and an American MP waved me over to the side. I got off the bike and thought I'd wait for Agnew to arrive. The MP comes over and says he's sorry but they're not letting in any civilians on bicycles or Hondas all day. "There's no way I can get to work then?" "No – take the day off," he said with a big grin. We both laughed. That was fine with me and I pedaled back to Tran Quy Cap to get my movie camera.

I went down Phung Khac Khoan to the street by the company villa and waited on the corner there. The cops were keeping traffic away from Ambassador Bunker's house. I could see red lights blinking far down the street as they approached. As I walked toward Hai Ba Trung the cars came roaring down Phung Khac Khoan. I got a little of it on camera. There were choppers landing and taking off from the American Embassy roof.

Saturday, August 29

On the way to work the back wheel of the bike started to wobble more than it had done. I knew about this and thought I would get it fixed tomorrow. As if in reply, it got worse. Then bam, the wheel broke in two and punctured the tire. The driver of a near-by cyclo got off and started to pick up the bike. I said, "No, that's OK." I locked the bike to a telephone pole girder and took a cyclo-mai the rest of the way.

In the evening George and I went to the Mass on his Honda. We sat at a table near the bar and the band. A couple of American girls come in. I introduced them to the military guys who were at our table. It was interesting to see how they interacted; American girls were at a premium here. Afterwards, we stopped by a place on Cach Mang where the French girl works.

Sunday, August 30

Took the bike to a repair shop in Cholon and got it fixed.

September 5 *The Saigon Post*:

Disabled Vets, MPs In Clash
Enraged disabled veterans Thursday wounded two American military policemen, seized two US jeeps and settled in for an all-night stand in dilapidated buildings in the Chinese section of the city while Vietnamese combat police surrounded the area. Disabled veterans have been demonstrating for months to get benefits from the government. Thursday's incident was the first time Americans became involved, however.

Sir Robert Thompson, the British guerilla warfare expert, came to HQMACV and commented that "Vietnam is a political problem of winning the allegiance of the people rather than a military problem of killing Viet Cong." Correct, in my view.

Thursday, September 10
In the evening George and I went to a bar on Tu Do, and shortly after we arrived a GI started an argument with the female owner. He yelled and swore at her and she said, "That is not the way to talk to a lady." "You're not a lady, you're a whore," he blurted out. When he had left, I said to her "Number 10 GI." George told me to be careful. I looked around and there were still a couple of GIs there. "Sometimes number 10 civilian too," I said.

There was a Honda accident at the corner of Cong Ly and Pasteur. A little boy was sitting on the curb, bandaged and bloody. He was sobbing and looked scared but people were there helping him. It probably scared him the more people looked at him.

Saturday, September 19
Evening with George to the Mass. We talked to an Army surgeon from Phu Bai. He told us that when he was treating a victim of a booby trap, the young soldier said, "What did I do to deserve this?" War is disgusting.

Another accident today. At the corner of Cong Ly and Gia Long a tri-Lambretta is turned on its side. An injured man is sitting on the street next to it. Police have arrived and there are already a few onlookers. As usual, there's a Honda involved. Maybe the Lambro had to swerve to avoid the Honda. There is blood and oil running on the asphalt. On the street under the Lambro there is a bloody bare footprint. It looks gruesome. There are also some spilled coins lying in the blood. A policeman starts methodically to measure off distances with a metal tape, jotting them down in his book.

Evening to Flora's but Thanh is not there. Talked to the bar owner about the grenade thrown by an ARVN guy. He said 18 people were wounded on Phanh Than Gian.

Ted says he may leave Sunday by ship to avoid Tan Son Nhut problem from the check he wrote to the Indians for black market money.

Wednesday, September 30

Progress reports today, always a pain. Took a walk in the sun around the "model hamlet," except this time on one of the smaller roads. Makes me want to get out in the field. There's something about the tropics, the lush greenery, the sounds of oriental music piercing the warm, calm, dank noon air. When this is all over, I thought, I'll buy some land and do with it as I want. Then I'll have paid for it with part of my soul – my soul will be in that very ground. Aren't we even born with our soul a part of the ground, like a plant or tree? It starts with the ground, shoots up temporarily for a brief life, then wilts and returns again; "Dust to dust."

Evening, went to the *Caroline Bar* in Dakao with George. There was a truck of armed security troops parked in front. George says "That's a bad sign." A French "mamasan" comes running out of Kim's Bar chasing two drunk ARVNs who hadn't paid their bill. This was a common occurrence as the soldiers feel that since they are doing the fighting they don't have to pay.

Thursday, October 1

On my way out to lunch I saw that an accident had happened on Plantation Road. Several Hondas were involved. A Vietnamese soldier was lying on the road and another leaned over him holding the victim's head up. Traffic jam trying to pass on the shoulders. A cop continuously blows a whistle and waves his arms. Incredibly an MP jeep drives up carrying a clown in the back – a man all dressed up like a circus clown. Irony – it's too much.

Monday, October 5

Things are pretty quiet here these past few days. No rockets or riots. They are having a trade fair in Saigon with all sorts of Vietnamese agricultural products, manufactured goods, and even antiques. Everything from raising hogs and poultry to information on rubber plantations and tractors. Part of it is a fairgrounds with magic shows and exhibitions such as motorcyclists riding inside a big cylinder. Also vitamins, shoes, silverware and Chinaware from the Ming Dynasty. It's incredible. I had a bit of time off so I took a look around and bought a montagnard crossbow from an exhibit on these mountain tribes.

Wednesday, October 7

MPC conversion today. Without prior notice, they suddenly change all MPC in order to catch black marketeers. Once in the HQMACV building you must change your MPC before leaving. Otherwise if you leave and come back you can't convert your money. So if you get inside the building and remember that you've left some MPC at home it's too bad. It becomes worthless. This is to prevent people from leaving the building, going downtown, buying up MPC from unauthorized people at low prices and returning. The PX and Snack Bar are closed all day.

Carl is bitching these days about Vietnamese overcharging him. A Tri-Lambretta driver at Tan Son Nhut charged him 50P instead of 40 as marked. Latest complaint is that he saw the new PACEX (Pacific Exchange) catalogue downtown on sale for 300P. "The Vietnamese can get it but I can't." It's really ludicrous to hear it. Some call it "Pacexification."

In the evening I went with some guys from the office to a bar on Nguyen Hue. One of the girls told us she has a house. "You come to my house, I have big house." She told us she used to sell fish in My Tho, but "No want to smell that number 10 smell again so have to work number one." I bought her a 200P tea instead of a 400P whisky. Another customer came in and she left to talk to him. At that point we left and went to a Tu Do nightclub to see the "Three Apples," a good Vietnamese singing group. Sort of a Vietnamese "Supremes."

Near closing time a potbellied American and a Korean soldier got into an argument. The Korean was waving his pistol in the air by the door. "Put your gun away," says the American, trying to make him back down. "Are you American? ARE YOU AMERICAN?" yells the Korean. Earl and I thought it would be a good idea to get out of there so we watched the scene from across the street. A couple of MP jeeps rolled up and we told them about the fight and the gun-waving Korean. They told us that they did not have jurisdiction in these cases. In a few minutes the two men left the bar together and parted shaking hands.

Friday, October 9

I went to see the magic show at the Agricultural Fair that Earl had raved about. There was an act where what appeared to be a woman was lying on her back on a table. There were knives stuck in her thighs and arms. The magician grabbed two or three of the knives and wiggled them, and the "flesh" wiggled too. Some sort of plastic? He took one of the knives out and showed it to the audience, letting one of them feel the blade. Then he spread a big sheet of paper over her abdomen which was "breathing" and "stabbed" her. "Blood" gushed out. He pulled what looked like guts from out of the abdominal cavity. Some in the audience screamed and some gasped. A few who knew the trick or had seen the act before were smiling. Price was 50P.

CHAPTER 12

Saturday, October 10

A new American girl from Data Processing was introduced around the department today. Her name was Ann. I got a good look at her. She's not bad, though a little pudgy. I wanted to ask her out, being Saturday night, but didn't feel as though I should press the issue that fast. Otherwise it was a pretty routine day with the usual statistics on security in the villages and a dull briefing in the CORDS conference room in the afternoon.

Sunday, October 11

Three o'clock in the afternoon and it's raining outside after a clear morning. The electricity went off, meaning no ceiling fans and my room gets very hot and mildewy – so close that you can smell your own lungs when you breathe out. Last night the water went off but I was lucky enough to have finished showering before.

Rain pings on the corrugated metal roof, timidly at first, then hard; the downpour comes all of a sudden, unannounced, like a bomb. I jumped. It gets louder and louder. Fortissimo! Like a raging storm at sea and to add to the racket, the kid next door is outside blowing a whistle at it. Everything is mildewed from the humidity. I had to take some books, those most prone to mildew, to work where it's air conditioned and less humid. The baby next door must have just been bathed for it was bawling. The "old man" came out to start up his Peugeot 403. He always just revs the engine over and over, then goes back inside.

Monday, October 12

In the evening I went to Caruso's. Jacqueline welcomed me with a sarcastic "*J'ne dirai rien*" (I won't say anything). She had invited me to the movies but I didn't feel like going so I told her I had been sick. Of course disbelief on her part. Nola came in with a boyfriend and they sat at a table in the back. She had cut her hair and Jacqueline didn't think at first that it was the same woman I had pointed out to her previously. "You know all the girls," she said, smiling. We played dice but as usual I lost and as usual she laughed at me. We nearly always had a good time talking – she sometimes standing behind the bar or sitting on a stool next to me when there were no customers.

At closing time I said *au revoir* to Jacqueline, went out into the Saigon night and climbed into a cyclo to go home. As the cyclo was rounding the big circle at the cathedral, I looked up and saw that the hands of the big clock on the Post Office building pointed to eleven o'clock. I heard the cyclo driver behind me say, "*Onze heures*" (eleven o'clock). "*Oui*," I replied, and for a fleeting instant I felt myself back in the French colonial days of 1950 – or even 1880.

Tuesday, October 13th

The days are becoming cooler and more cloudy, but still partly sunny during the day. High temperatures are often falling short of 90 which is actually chilly in Saigon. The heavy rain continues however, almost every day at 6:00 p.m. like clockwork.

Wednesday, October 14

No rain today for a change. Coming out of the USAHAC library, as I was getting on the back of a Honda, shots rang out from down toward Hong Thap Tu, about five or six of them. I jumped off the Honda and crouched behind a parked car. Several Vietnamese on motorbikes also pulled over and ran for cover. A group of Vietnamese soldiers didn't look too concerned so I dismissed it as random shooting. However, just then a cop, brandishing a smoking pistol, came wheeling by on the back of a Honda chasing someone.

Here so far from home, it must be this daily grind that produces a dizzying reflection of self, often occurring as one walks alone. Another strange phenomenon is the morbid interpretation of a passage in a book. The brain somehow short circuits to a tragedy involving one's family. Strange things happen to the mind under these circumstances and one has constantly to exercise good control over one's mental self.

Friday, October 16
After work I got a ride home with Roger and the new girl Ann. She seemed pretty hyper and tense. "Are you married?" she asked me. "Not yet," said Roger, answering for me. "Thank you Roger," she said. We let her off at the company villa. Maybe there's no chance with her, I thought.

A new army guy at HQ asks, after a loud burst from one of our near daily thunder and lightning storms, "How do you tell if it's an incoming rocket, or just thunder?" Everyone of course laughed. Dave rushed out of his corner cubicle to say, "For one thing there's no shrapnel." A major said, "You'll know if we all dive under the desks."

Wednesday, October 21
An amusing incident today. A lieutenant colonel, on his way out of the men's room, having apparently performed his bowel function in minimal time, got the attention of the little Vietnamese cleaning woman who was waiting to clean out the toilets. Grinning at the officer she says, "Fini shit huh? NUMBAH ONE!"

Friday, October 23
I ventured to talk to Ann and asked her out to lunch at the Mass. I was surprised when she readily agreed. We had a couple of rounds of beer and then ordered lunch. The service was slow and she hardly stopped worrying out loud about getting back to work on time. She even said that we could skip lunch. A bit over the top, I thought. I convinced her that it was OK to stay. During our conversation she said she hadn't yet seen one guy here who turned her on. "What about me?" I asked. "You look married," she said. Once again she seemed to be on the hyper side.

That evening Earl and I go, in spite of the rain, to a couple of bars for a few beers and to look at the local talent. The first place we go is called "*147.*"

It's owned by Americans, and the customers are all American civilians. The girls wear white dress uniforms that have tags with their name and number.

Earl told me about a girl from Tay Ninh who had answered his ad for a Vietnamese language tutor. She came to Saigon, moved in with him, then made a duplicate key and stole all his stuff.

Saturday, October 24

Ann parades around the office like she wants something. She comes up to my desk, puffing on a cigarette, and after some idle chatter about the stuffed cobra and mongoose on my desk, she comes out with, "A good rub down would sure feel good – a strong scotch too."

The rest of the day I could only think about how I could manage to seduce this woman.

She left work early, so I phoned her at the company villa to ask her out. "I would love to but I have an engagement." She didn't seem to care about missing work that afternoon, notwithstanding her intense worry over the duration of lunch yesterday.

I said, "You mentioned something about a scotch?" trying once again.

"I'll take a rain check," she said.

Sunday, October 25

After a couple cups of coffee in my room, I decided to bike around by the villa and see if Ann was there, although I wasn't sure that it was a good idea. Nice day, although hot. At the company villa I smiled and nodded at the maids. I walked upstairs and knocked on a likely door on the third floor. I hadn't expected her to be there so when I heard her coming to the door I was pleasantly surprised. After amenities, she said, "I could sure use a beer." But where to find some? We tried the dining room but it was locked. I asked the maids but they said, "No beer." I then volunteered to go to a shop across the street to get some. I was a little shaky – from high hormone level and also being a bit on the spot. I bought four beers and a loaf of bread, which later turned out to have bugs in it. We went up to the villa roof, talked and drank our beers. Beethoven's Seventh Symphony was coming over the little transistor radio that I had set on the railing.

I was thinking all the time what we could do together to lead into more intimate relations – a transition.

"Hey, how would you like to go on a trip in a sampan up the canals off the Saigon River? I've done it before and it's a lot of fun." I could hardly believe I had said that. "That sounds great," she said, and off we went on a cyclo-mai to the river front. I was showing off my knowledge of the city to her.

There are dozens of sampans for hire at the river front. We took one that looked good and climbed aboard. An older Vietnamese woman with the usual conical hat started up the outboard motor. Her young daughter was constantly engaged in bailing out the old wooden tub that, like so many in Vietnam, had the 'evil eye' painted on each side of the bow. We threaded our way along, putt-putting through these common sewers. The further up the canal we went the blacker and filthier the water got. We were squeezed in on both sides by rows of wood shacks on piles built out over the water. Several times the propeller got jammed by garbage so we had to stop the motor, lift up the prop and pick out the offending wet plastic bag or other hunk of floating detritus.

This intricate network of canals whose banks were lined with wooden shantytowns branched off from the Saigon River through the city in every direction.

Some of these stilt houses had a stall 'toilet' that overhung the water. Scant privacy was provided by a few boards. Occasionally a mooning shitter in one of these crude outhouses, black pajama bottoms dropped, would turn, look and smile at the passing sampan. Not far away, others on their balconies or porches were fishing for their evening meal.

Everyone ran out to look down at us to see the foreigners in a sampan, whole families crowding at the doors and windows of their shacks to laugh, flash toothy smiles, and wave.

We saw a man sitting in a porch chair in front of one of the shacks. He almost looked like a round-eye. "This would be a good place to hide," I said. "Why would you want to hide?" I didn't answer. We went as far as possible on the narrowing canal and then headed back.

Rather than take the sampan all the way to the docks, we hopped off onto the river bank at the Saigon Botanical Gardens from where it's an easy walk home.

An earlier tourist brochure states:

For the tourist who cannot put up with noise or commotion of the city and who longs for green grass and trees, the Botanical Gardens are an ideal place for quiet relaxation and fresh air. Lazy ponds full of water lilies seem to be the proper setting for the beauty of the Vietnamese girls. Inside are broad avenues and narrow paths winding through green lawns.

We returned to the villa roof patio and opened a couple more beers. We were getting chummier all the time.

Suddenly she said, "If we become lovers – that won't affect our relationship at work, will it?" I was a bit surprised at this direct question and was getting ready to answer when she said, "I'd like to sleep this afternoon – preferably with you."

In a few minutes she looked at me, smiled and asked, "Anyone sleepy?"

Downstairs, she climbed on the back fender of my bicycle. Both of us laughed at the spectacle as I pedaled over to Tran Quy Cap. People were gawking at us – an unusual sight we were.

Once in the room, she started to undress immediately, as if we had already been together many times. "I just wanted to break the ice," she would later explain when I kidded her about it.

Monday, October 26

When we awoke at five o'clock in the morning it was raining hard. Suddenly she said, "Are you happy?" I admitted that it wasn't easy for me to just say 'yes' to this question. She reached across to hold my hand. I said, "You *are* cuddly aren't you?" She snuggled up to me. I walked her back to the company villa. It was still just 6:00. I decided to stay awake the rest of the day.

The only contact I had with her at work was in a meeting. After work she said some military guys had invited her to swim tomorrow. Jealousy already rears its head.

Time and *Newsweek* both had articles about our work on the HES. Nixon cited the recent figures that 92.8 per cent of South Vietnam's 17 million people now live "under government protection." Nixon claimed that we could now "negotiate from strength."

There were newspaper articles on another side of life in Saigon:

Vietnam Guardian:

LOOKING AROUND

Big night for flowers

Three rappers (sic) are being held for prosecution and another is being tracked down by police authorities, it was reported.

The men involved were in two separate cases of rape.

Sources said the first case took place Saturday night when a bar girl on the way home met two male friends who invited her to a drink with them.

The girl accepted their invitation, but when they finished drinking, the curfew hour was near and they convinced the girl that she ought to sleep overnight at their house.

During the night, the pair took advantage of the dark and shipped (sic) into her mosquito net then forced themselves upon her sexually pollinating her "flower."

After the pair had relieved their pressure and fallen into sleep, the girl escaped from the house and ran out to the street shouting for help.

Patrol police came and after hearing her claim, launched a net to round up the suspects, but one of them had escaped already. Only one suspect was taken into custody for further questioning.

Tuesday, October 27

I asked Ann, as she was looking over paperbacks by my desk, "What are you doing for dinner?" We agreed to meet at the Splendid at 8 o'clock. "Write down the address so I can show it to the cab driver," she said. She was new in town.

When she arrived she was wearing a white pants plus blouse thing like a towel in texture. It looked good on her.

"I'm looking for an apartment," she said, as she read out loud the apartment ads in the *Saigon Post*. She was in a good mood and we held hands. "I feel at ease and relaxed around you – I can be myself – that doesn't usually happen," she said.

"Do you want to go out and see a show? But I don't have much money." She said, "We can go home – we don't have to go out."

We rode home with her on the back of the bicycle again. People do double takes.

Not much sleep that night.

Wednesday, October 28

It is raining hard all the time during the early morning hours. When she got up she was in too much of a hurry for my liking. "Miserable bitch," I said, half kidding, half serious. "Do you mean that?" she said, as she slipped back into yesterday's clothes.

"How long has it been since you've been to bed? I just can't believe I turn you on that much." She couldn't see why I was so attracted to her. "You're really way out of my league – good-looking, better education." I assured her that she was very attractive and that, "Apparently you *do* turn me on." I had to force that phrase out a bit, not because it wasn't true, but because I didn't feel comfortable with the expression.

I got up, dressed and walked her part way to the villa. Suddenly she starts to run. I catch up with her, and then we run hand in hand. "See you at work," I yell as she enters the villa. I didn't hear her say anything in reply.

Thursday, October 29

I got soaked to the bone after pedaling all five miles to Headquarters in a tropical downpour. At the office I poured the rain water out of my shoes and took off my shirt and undershirt. One of the women was shocked at this behavior.

Friday, October 30

I received the 'green' (two $100 bills) today, so could make a transaction with the Indians on Tu Do. As I was leaving the office I talked to Ann but, as usual, we are constrained to pretend there is nothing going on between us. Concealment – was it Ann who had engineered it? Did she think it would make her seem more attractive to me if there were the forbidden element? It was one of those games. She was always the one who strove to keep our relationship secret, or so it seemed; yet she amused herself within this sham secrecy. "There's going to be a party at the company villa tonight," she said, but I said I didn't want to go. "I'll see you tomorrow since you'll probably get involved in the party tonight anyway." At that she slammed the safe drawer shut and walked off.

I biked downtown to the Indians' shop, but before transacting, decided to go to the villa and call her. "It's hard to converse at work," I said. "I'm sorry," she said, and good relations returned. "I don't have to meet you at the villa, I can meet you somewhere else," she said. "Yes, but the trouble is you don't know anything; I mean you don't know where any places are." She laughed. So we decided to meet in front of the villa.

The 'transaction' was accompanied by somewhat more '007'-ism. From the glass showcases, one of the Indians pulled out all sorts of miscellaneous items for me to look at while I was waiting: face cloths, soap, batteries, etc. while the other man, behind a screen at the back of the shop, gathered together the stack of Piasters and MPC. This time the rates were 410 Piasters to the dollar and $1.45 MPC for $1.00 green.

Earl and I met, as planned, at the Kon Tiki Bar, but the 'sexy dancer show,' we were told, is only Wednesdays and Saturdays. There was a band and a singer though, so we stayed anyway. During one number, a young girl came running around, making sweeps of the floor with a rolled-up newspaper lit at the end. She swept it side to side under all the chairs and tables. "What the hell's *that* for?" we wondered. Earl said, "Either to scare away the evil spirits – or the cockroaches."

I took a taxi to the company villa and there in front was Ann sitting, glass in hand, with the watchman.

She said she didn't want to leave the party yet. Finally, after many tries, she talked me into coming upstairs to the party – separately. She gave me a little kiss, wiped the lipstick off my face, and started up the stairs. I said, "If I'm not up in a few minutes you'll know I went home." "Oh come on," she said. But I turned away and headed home. I couldn't see subjecting myself to a miserable evening with no possibility of getting her out of there. So, hurting inside, I walked home, knowing I was probably breaking everything off. I couldn't sleep and couldn't read – just lay there and worried about it. Finally, at about midnight I fell asleep.

I had been asleep about an hour when I vaguely heard knocks at the door and someone calling me at the window. I got up, not knowing what it was. Suddenly I recognized her voice. She had left the party 'bombed,' in her words, walked to my villa and had somehow managed to climb the seven-foot high, spiked gate – and with a wine glass in one hand! Incredible.

Saturday, October 31
In the morning after coffee together she took a taxi to MACV. I wanted to ride my bike so I was late but she covered for me.

Lots of rain these past few days but soon the rainy season will be over. Tomorrow is National Day here and, as usual, everyone predicts rocket attacks on Saigon. One hears a blast now and then but seldom is any clarification forthcoming. Usually you just ask at work, "Did anyone hear an explosion last night?"

Sunday, November 1
National Day, flags are out. Ann and I went apartment hunting for her. She keeps trying to talk me into extending for six months. "Why don't you re-up?"

Monday, November 2
Three or four rockets hit Saigon Monday shortly after midnight, according to AFVN but we didn't hear them. Two hit near the Saigon Market and killed five Vietnamese civilians. That same night, we heard a plane overhead, and I remarked to Ann that, "The last time I heard that plane Saigon had just been rocketed."

Tuesday, November 3
After work we took a taxi to Maxim's nightclub at 13 Tu Do. Their ad in the newspapers:

BEAUTY AT MAXIM'S

Vietnam is the birthplace of beauties. Have you seen a typical one while here? Miss Mong Tuyen, Vietland's most beautiful TV star, portrays "I am the Queen" and "A Mad Woman Looking For Her Son" at
MAXIM'S
SUMMER SHOW

The usual Scotch and water for her, bourbon and seven for me. I had trouble keeping her there. She said she was tired and wanted to go home. When I asked how much the drinks were, she got upset because I wouldn't have another one. They were 800 for the first, and 550 for each additional. "I see we have different ideas of life," she said.

The program, printed in Vietnamese, English, and Chinese on expensive card stock with a bright red cover announcing "VIETNAM SHOW" listed the 14 different shows. One of them was bilingually entitled, "Je Sais, Malaguena," (I know, Malaguena).

At 9:00 the long-awaited show finally started with a number listed in English as "Moon-shaped Hat Dance." Following this were a series of various songs and dances: a solo by the "International singer Mario," a dance called "Afro Ritual," a female solo, "Thanks to Love," and a Vietnamese dance entitled "Evening Prayers."

Then there followed, incongruously, a circus.

Ann had enjoyed the show until this point. She reached over to hold my hand and to tell me she wanted to go home. We left and went back to my place.

Wednesday, November 4

Next morning we argued as she was leaving. "Will you see me to the gate?" she said. I mumbled something which didn't augur for much activity. "I'm tired of getting shitty answers all the time," she yelled. "I don't want to see you again." She had a real bitchy side that started to wear away at my feelings towards her.

There were a few rain drops today but not enough to keep down the dust.

Ann went by herself to look at an apartment she had seen in the paper. She came to my desk to tell me this and then as she walked away she turned around and stuck out her tongue puckishly at me. Maybe this meant that she had wanted – or expected – to be asked out afterwards. But she had admitted to being tired and had said she was going to "put this little girl to bed early."

Thursday, November 5

No rain again today. Dusty. I felt that I could no longer stand the tearing at my psyche of this crazy affair, always being conscious of where Ann is and who she is talking to.

Friday, November 6

In the evening after work several of us at the office went over to the Mass. I had to bike over there right away so the prima donna Ann wouldn't be there without someone to escort her. We played the one-armed bandits and watched the show that starred a sexy Filipino girl dancer.

Afterwards we went to an open-air Vietnamese restaurant on Cach Mang. The toilets, which were really outhouses, were pretty filthy. Ann had to go, but after one look at the inside of the outhouse she refused. I told her to "Go ahead and take a leak for Christ sakes." She did.

We had 'one kind of beef' and eel soup. Later we went to a place called *Phuong's* where a group was playing Hawaiian songs.

Going home, she took a cyclo-mai while I rode my bicycle alongside, holding on to the cyclo-mai with one hand.

November 12 *The Saigon Post*:

Saigon Defense Screen Boosted

Saigon, US infantry troops have moved to within 15 miles of downtown Saigon for the first time in 11 months to help protect the capital from Communist infiltration, spokesmen and military sources said Wednesday.

Soldiers from the 25th Division in the past 10 days or two weeks have been helping set up a protective screen on the eastern approaches to Saigon, the sources said.

US intelligence sources said Communist forces have been breaking up into small units for the past several months in the Saigon area, and are expected to try to move terror teams into the capital as part of an overall Communist plan to revert to guerrilla warfare in South Vietnam.

The move back into the Saigon periphery reverses a US policy of allowing South Vietnamese soldiers to supply all the protection for the city.

Wednesday, November 18

I've been sick for almost a week with a sore throat and a cough that sometimes I can hardly stop. I almost threw up from coughing. It takes colds and infections a lot longer to heal over here in this climate. I have to get all my shots over again. Even tetanus, which I otherwise wouldn't have needed, but I cut myself on my bicycle. As a result, I had not wanted to see Ann for a while, but at noon today I got friendly again and after lunch we walked over to the Buddhist Temple near MACV. We go up the Pagoda steps and look at the huge gold Buddha. It's hot and we sweat a lot. I told Ann not to do any cuddling while we are near the pagoda.

Saturday, November 21

At 6:00 Ann comes over to my desk and I ask, "Where are you going to eat tonight?" She shrugs her shoulders and says, "I don't know," then she leaves. I feel lonely and can't think of anything else. On the news when I got home from work, the radio reported that we had bombed SAM (Surface to Air Missile) sites in North Vietnam. My first thought was that we're in for some more rockets.

Sunday, November 22

She came over to my room at 9 a.m. She said, "You stood me up last night – you said you'd bring a bottle of wine over." I had asked her, but she didn't seem all that enthusiastic.

We took a taxi to 'bicycle city' in Cholon to get a Honda brand bicycle for her.

Monday, November 23

I rode my bike to work, encountering two APCs of the MP battalion on my way through the MACV gate. Yesterday there was a jeep lying upside down on Pasteur Street with gas dripping out of the tank.

Although I arrived a bit late at the office, I assumed that Ann had marked me on time.

After dinner that evening we rode our bikes around the dark Saigon Streets. "There's a nightclub on the top floor of that building," I said, pointing to a tall building on the traffic circle. "I told you there are lots of interesting places we'll have to go to around here."

She hollered, "Yes, you'll have to re-up so we can see them all."

Soon she got tired of the cycling and said, "I'm about to call it quits."

We went to her new apartment she had rented. She busied herself with little chores like washing her hairbrush and just walked past me without any eye contact, let alone romanticism. Out of the blue she says, "I'm going to bed." I departed without a word. The neighboring dogs barked. "Damned dogs," I muttered.

There was some artillery that evening, probably on account of the recent bombing raids over North Vietnam. There were also many new check points and more soldiers than usual.

Tuesday, November 24

I got up early to meet Ann at the villa where she catches the bus but she wasn't there as I had half expected.

As I biked to work, I saw her on Cong Ly on the bus. At a red light I rode up to the bus and banged on her window. She jumped and others laughed. "Thanks for waiting for me!" I yelled. "I didn't know," she shouted through the glass window.

At HQ, she wrote me a nice apology note.

After work it was raining so I took a taxi to Ann's place. When I walk in she says "Hi, baby," and is in a good mood.

Wednesday, November 25

I stayed home all day sick. I had picked up a cold or the flu. All I had to eat was a little spaghetti. Earl came by and asked if I was all right. He said that Ann was concerned. "I'll call back and tell her that you're OK."

In the evening, the owner knocked on my door and asked *"Est-ce que vous êtes malade monsieur?"* (Are you sick monsieur?). Apparently they noticed that I had stayed home that day. He asked if I had seen a doctor, and if I needed anything.

I had expected Ann to come by but she never did. That was just about it, I thought.

At night a rocket landed nearby. I jumped out of bed and made a leap for the bathroom. At 1:30 a second explosion rocked the area and the droning of the rocket spotter plane could be heard afterwards.

Thursday, November 26
Didn't make it to work – my cough was too bad.

Around 2:00 Earl came over and we bullshitted a while. Earl said Ann was concerned again. I cursed her out and said, "If she was really concerned she would have come over last night."

Friday, November 27
Again stayed home sick. The usual hacking when I got up. Ann came by in the afternoon. I was sitting on the edge of the bed with only an undershirt on. I reprimanded her for not coming by. She replied by slipping into bed. She asked me if I would come over to her place later. I agreed but didn't think it was right since she hadn't come to see me when I was sick.

The family at my villa insisted they feed me and brought me a tray with two fried eggs, bread, lentil and meat soup, and three green oranges. It was good of them. The soup smelled strong and oriental. It was exactly the same smell as the cooking odors of their family meals that wafted their way into my room every evening at dinner time.

I slept a bit to regain energy for the evening. Now it's raining again.

I cycled over to Ann's. As I walked in, she said, "Hi baby!" It was dark except for a light next to her bed.

Saturday, November 28
Getting out of bed at 7:30 I had to cough my throat out. A shower didn't help so I said the hell with it and went back to bed. Around noon Ann showed up in her pink pant suit outfit, a long coat buttoning down the front.

She got upset because she had to ask me several times if I was coming over later, said I was spoiled and she'd have to get someone else. She left at 1:30 on her bicycle.

After I had a bite to eat, I put on my sport coat and walked over to her place. She got really POed that I had eaten already. Finally, after much venomous garbage, she just threw up her hands saying, "Get out of my house!" but not looking at me. This I did angrily, gathering up my coat left

162

from a previous night. Walked home. I cut up some oranges the owners had left and read some in a travel book on India. Tomorrow, I'll pick up *Les Nouvelles du Dimanche* and go down to the docks. I wondered what Ann did after I had left and what she'll do tomorrow or Monday.

Sunday, November 29

She did it – she was here at 8:45. Knocking on the door she yelled, "Let me in! Wake up!" But I was too groggy. "I'm too tired, I want to sleep." She kept it up for quite a while. I said, "I'll stop over later." "No, you won't stop over later."

Finally she quit, as a loud plane drowned out her efforts. I went back to sleep for half an hour or so then got up and made coffee. The usual hacking wasn't quite so bad. Just as I was drinking my coffee, she knocks on the door again. I yelled, "Ann? Wait a minute," and let her in.

Later, we took a taxi to the Meyerkord BOQ for lunch, then walked down the street to the Central Market. We stopped at the fortune tellers by the Hindu temple, looked at Christmas cards at the stalls on Le Loi, bought two Vietnamese paintings of the Mekong Delta on Nguyen Hue, then took a taxi home.

The kids outside the villa made some comments in French as the two of us went to my room.

Friday, December 4

Bike to work on time. Ann said to come over and pick up my Listerine (for my cough) and my book. I asked her what she did last night. She said, "I stayed home, thanks to you. I wish you had told me – I could have made other plans." Life is complicated with her!

Saturday, December 5

Bike to work, but the chain slips off just before the bridge over the canal. I put it back on and started to ride but it slipped off again, so I wheeled the bike across the bridge and locked it to a telephone pole, one of those metal girder ones. Finally got a bus to work, arriving about 8:15. I walk in with hard expression on my face. I take the computer printout off my desk and the rubber band breaks and snaps on the cut I got from fixing the bike. On top of that, I had seen Brown sitting at his desk without a tie. I threw the deck across the room to the wastebasket and IBM cards fly all over. George and others laugh as I curse. Later one of the majors and I talk about stupidity of this "tie rule."

At noon I went with George to a local Mexican restaurant. He told me that he had asked Ann out for dinner tonight. I had no comment on this but it was not welcome news.

Ann didn't talk to me all day and only incidentally before the project meeting at five o'clock. At six, just as George is leaving work, I say to him, "Take care." He replies, "The whole thing is off," so we go together to recover my bike. And it is still there! Some teenagers who were watching help me put the chain back on and I ride the bike to my place.

Sunday, December 6

It was a beautiful, sunny day. I pumped air into the front tire, enough so I could ride it. I'm ambivalent about going to Ann's – she may be sick. I pedaled to the city center in spite of the wobbly back wheel.

On Le Loi I noticed a patent medicine man, purporting to be a dentist, working from a little stand on the sidewalk. With clever patter and sleight of hand, he convinces the onlookers that his magic potion in small vials can cure a painful toothache. Orders come in from all sides of the crowd, hands reaching out 50 Piaster notes.

The quack dentist quickly wraps each small vial in a little square of newspaper, all the while pocketing the cash and keeping up his patter.

Other sidewalk vendors nearby yell at the 'dentist' for standing in front of their concessions. After fifteen minutes of argument, he picks up his little table and moves it twenty feet away. Business is still good though. A father has brought his little son for dental treatment. The old man shells out the 50P and walks away the proud owner of a miracle medicine.

I bought a French newspaper, then rode my bike to the docks of the Saigon River. There was the *London Advocate* from Copenhagen. I was able to board her and look around. Had tea in the dockside café and relaxed. No one knows where I am, I thought. On the way back I stopped at the *Guillaume Tell* for an *omelette nature, salade de tomates,* and *café au lait.* The restaurant was advertised in the newspapers:

Restaurant Guillaume Tell, 32-34 Rue Trinh Minh The.

French cuisine, charming atmosphere, Mme Madeleine Leccia Welcomes You. Tel 91. 456.

Monday, December 7

In the office Ann didn't say anything much to me in the morning but I joked with her as I took my Phoenix papers out of the safe. She looked to be friendly enough and asked me for lunch, but I said I had to wait for the tape that the computer guys were making for me. She walked away without a word.

George handed in his resignation this morning, a sad day for me. In the afternoon there was another Progress meeting. Life goes on.. Thursda

Saturday, December 12

No contact with Ann for some time now, aside from brief chats at the office. But today I decided to break the ice and talk to her and we agreed to go out to dinner. However, I thought the evening would be easier, in view of recent arguments, if I invited a friend of mine, Bill, who works on the first floor of the MACV HQ building. He's a fun guy who I went bar hopping with once in a while.

The three of us went to dinner at the Brink BOQ (named after US Army Brigadier General Francis Brink). As we drive in the taxi past the US Embassy, the intersection of Hai Ba Trung and Thong Nhut is barricaded. There are helmeted NPFF toting rifles and wearing flak jackets, standing in front. At another major check point on Hai Ba Trung we are stopped by a policeman and an NPFF guy with rifle. They don't look any too friendly and ask if we are civilians. They wanted to see our IDs. Finally they are satisfied and let us proceed. At the Brink we talk about possible anti-American demonstrations.

Ann says to Bill, "I've been trying to get him (meaning me) to move in with me ever since I got here." She also said, half jokingly, that she thinks she's pregnant. Anything to get attention. Afterwards we all went to a nightclub near Earl's place.

Memos circulated at HQ warned us to stay away from Cholon. There were anti-American riots there because an American had shot a Vietnamese boy by accident in Qui Nhon. It was in the papers.

Vietnam Guardian:

STUDENTS SQUARE OFF WITH POLICE

Police and an estimated 200 students lobbed tear gas grenades and Molotov cocktails at each other for over three hours here Saturday night in an exchange sparked by the fatal shooting of a high school student in Qui Nhon last Monday.

Joint National Police and Police Field Forces (combat police) sealed off the Minh Mang student center near the boundary between Saigon and the Cholon section of the city where the students were holed up.

The students said that efforts to set four US vehicles afire on Hai Ba Trung and Le Loi streets were abortive. However authorities report that one USAID car parked on Cao Thang Street was burned during the night. A note found nearby said the incident was "In retaliation for the murders of high school student in Qui Nhon and two other Vietnamese youths."

Last week the student was shot and killed across the street from a parked US military truck in Qui Nhon where a GI said he had fired warning shots to scare off pilferers trying to get at the load of C-rations on the vehicle.

Two days of rioting followed the incident.

Saigon Student Union president Huynh, talking to newsmen in his headquarters across the street from the scene of Saturday night's incident said there would be stronger measures taken unless the two American soldiers who killed the youth in Qui Nhon are turned over to Vietnamese authorities.

The students said they intended to march on the US Embassy to burn in effigy Ambassador Elsworth Bunker and President Nixon.

It was also in the papers back in the States.

The San Francisco Chronicle, December 14, 1970 headlined:

Boy's Death Stirs Vietnam Hatred

I was outraged. I vowed to continue to free as many students as I could and I would send the memo and the letter. I would have to type them myself.

Tuesday, December 15

I left work early to meet Ann at her doctor's office, but I couldn't find it – she hadn't given me the exact address. I was angry and just went to the Splendid and then home.

Wednesday, December 16

At the office Ann says sarcastically, "I'm sure you did," and "I can believe it," when I told her I had tried for an hour to find that doctor.

In the afternoon she says she found the doctor's right address. She wrote me a note saying, "Everything should be all right," and asked me what I was doing for dinner. I told her we were going to the Mass with the military. She didn't say anything one way or the other.

Thursday, December 17

Ann was not too friendly so I went with Earl to the airport for lunch. I had Chinese soup and a club sandwich. They played *Your Cheatin' Heart*, *I Gotta Get Outta This Place*, and the perennial *Sugar, Sugar*. I am looking forward to my time off next week.

Ann left early at five, supposedly to see the doctor. She tried to bring me a note earlier, but George was at my desk. She made an annoyed clicking sound and turned around on her heels. I rolled my eyes. George says, "Well that's the price you have to pay."

"So far, it's cheaper than buying a girl," I answered.

Friday, December 18

At noon I went with Ann for lunch at the Mass. She had told me in the morning that everything was all right. She said it matter-of-factly, as though this was releasing me, which it was. She said, "You weren't there when I needed you last night."

The Horne BOQ on Plantation Road was hit by a time bomb that supposedly went off in the water cooler and killed the duty officer and a Vietnamese. George said he was watching a movie at the Mass when they stopped it and asked all physicians to immediately go to emergency at Third Field Hospital. That must have been for the grenade that went off in back of the Missouri BOQ. At night I was kept awake by shots.

Saturday, December 19

I got POed because of cigarette butts on the floor under my desk. I swept it all out into the middle of the room. "Goddamned pigpen!" I yelled, and Ann walked away smiling. Dave laughed and said, "He's having another one of his mornings."

Viet Cong and North Vietnamese broadcasts called for "greatly increased offensive action" against American and South Vietnamese troops and military installations.

Two rockets hit near my villa this morning at 2:00. They woke me up. On AFVN just after the long beep that preceded the news, "Rockets hit SAIgon," intoned the military announcer.

How strange that Ted is gone. He had finally been sent out of the country for his black market fiasco. Somehow, just knowing that he was here held down a corner, so to speak.

Monday, December 21

In the morning Ann comes over as I'm taking a shower. The radio was on AFVN and was playing some popular songs. We start getting cozy and suddenly she calls attention to what they are playing, and says nostalgically, "*Bridge over Troubled Water*, baby," recalling one of 'our' songs.

Later we ride our bicycles and look at shops on Le Loi. We stop to have a drink at a sidewalk stand. She goes across street and picks up a chunk of ice from a garbage can, brings it back and puts it into her drink. I could not believe it.

We leave our bikes at my place, then take a taxi to Tu Do and change money at the Indians' shop. Went back to her apartment. The Christmas tree lights blink through the night.

Tuesday, December 22

Went to an antique shop near the Central Market. A Buddhist funeral was taking place across the street and I watched warily. There was a big, black van, inside of which I saw a coffin. There were plenty of onlookers, mostly women, children, and a few old men. The men and women were of strong peasant stock and had the imprint of many years of labor on their faces. On the sidewalk next to the van was a crude wooden table set with two glasses of wine, a bowl of fruit, some flowers, and incense (joss) sticks. An old woman fed pieces of cardboard to a small fire, causing many bits of ash to float in the smoky air. Several people climbed into the back of the van and sat on benches on either side of the wooden coffin. One of them was a woman holding a little child. The woman was sobbing, bending back and forth over the coffin, almost banging her head against the wood in agony. Her face was distorted in pain. It was a terrible sight. A half-hour later it was all over and the van drove away with a little 3-wheeled vehicle following. Everyone disbursed. A woman carefully wrapped up the things on the table and dumped out the remaining liquid from the glasses into the smoldering fire. Some people still eating were fanning the ashes away from their food with conical hats. Business resumed as usual.

I crossed the street feeling rather humble and ostentatious as a large American among the local crowd.

Later I biked over to Ann's but she isn't there. I was going to ask her to dinner at USAID. I go there by myself feeling a little lonely. Had steak and then went home. My cough is just about beaten now and I can control it for the first time.

A little bit more outgoing than usual this evening. A few minutes ago there was a volley of five or six shots a few blocks away. Now the radio is playing *Silent Night* and the guns still boom. There are no glass windows in my room, so there is no problem of possible shattered glass. The open lattices allow plenty of air to pass through.

Wednesday, December 23

At MACV the following note was passed around warning of student demonstrations:

EXPEDITE!

MEMO

- *Exercise extreme caution in driving to Vung Tau during the holiday season.*
- *Student demonstrations are planned for midnight on the 24th and probably on the 31st, New Year's Eve. The word is to be careful downtown or in any crowds.*

- *Recommended that you do not go to midnight mass at the cathedral in Kennedy Square.*
- *Remember to keep doors locked in automobiles.*
- *Recommended that you refrain from large gatherings; in other words, stay out of crowds.*

This information should be disseminated to all employees.

I thought immediately of Thanh's brother. Would he be among the leaders once again?

Later that evening, there was an incessant rattling noise from next door. The kid here got a toy machine gun for Christmas. In Vietnam of all places! The sound of it is getting on my nerves.

Thursday, December 24

In the morning I rode out on my bike, crossed the bridge on Truong Minh Giang and saw an antique shop back in an alleyway. These places in Saigon were always interesting. The Vietnamese were anxious to trade their antiques for hard currency in these times of war. There were *objets d'art* displayed on a wooden staircase, and a cupboard containing blue Chinaware. Further up the street I spotted a handicraft shop in a narrow alley. The whole family is engaged in creating lacquerware: trays, coffee tables, vases, etc. The son, six years old, sits on the floor and wraps the finished piece in pages of an old newspaper. It's so professional the way he places the object in the middle of a sheet of paper, makes the folds, using his feet to hold down the nearest corner, and a pair of pliers for the farthest one. He takes a rubber band, stretches it back and forth with several quick pulls, then slips it over the side of the package. I buy two carved mahogany figures of mother and child. They asked 6,000 but I offer 4,000 and we settled on five.

When I arrived home, there was a small envelope under my door. Inside was a handwritten note:

My Dear
I feel
sad and miss you, that I

want you to come and see
me (IF YOU CAN)

Love,
Thanh

What did she want, I wondered. It must be about the student riots. I went to the Tokyo Bar at 39, Tu-Do. *Your pleasure and relaxation in our service*, reads their ad in the *Saigon Post*.

As I walk in, she calls out excitedly, "*Ong rau!*" as she sometimes calls me, and we sit together in a booth. I asked her if her brother was involved in the demonstrations. She says he was but he was not arrested. She says she is still in love with me. Tells me how lonely she is, and somehow I believe her. She was even more animated than usual. Cleopatra couldn't have been more seductive.

"You must help us again," she pleaded, squeezing my hand and looking me intently in the face. How could I refuse?

"All right, I will," I said. She smiled that smile you couldn't resist. I told her I would send the memo and letter about students being arrested and tortured that I had promised. She hugged me and thanked me. "My brother will thank you too," she said with tears in her eyes. I returned to my room. I wondered what Ann's reaction would be to my evening with Thanh.

Friday, December 25
Earl and I have Chinese dinner in the *Peacock Restaurant* at 60, Nguyen Van Thinh. The Christmas throngs and noise are almost unbearable. From the cathedral all the way down Tu Do past the Caravelle is a solid mob of people.

We then go to the back garden of the *Continental Palace*. Nice tropical setting.

LA DOLCE VITA
RESTAURANT
Offers you its Italian specialties
and its famous pizza in a rustic
atmosphere and charming surrounding.

Address: CONTINENTAL Hotel
132 Tu Do – Tel ; 90.157

Saturday, December 26
As I was drinking coffee in my room, Ann arrives and announces in an irritated tone:

"Here are your Christmas presents you didn't bother to come and get," she said. "We're through. I'm not going to rely on you anymore." She had no comment on the laquerware gift I had given her.

"When was it any different?"

"It was once," she said. "You just didn't appreciate it."

"I couldn't come, I had to see a friend," I said. "It was an emergency."

"Yours or hers?" she replied sarcastically.

I explained the situation to her, how I had "freed" Thanh's brother and fellow student anti-war protesters who were being arrested and tortured by the Saigon regime. I told her about the Phoenix abuses in the field and that I would send memos about it.

She seemed not to be really listening and suddenly said, "Do you want to come over for a beer later?"

"OK," I said, without much enthusiasm.

It was nearly two o'clock in the afternoon when I arrived at her place. We drank a couple of beers, and, for just this festive time of year, sat like an old married couple listening to the Bob Hope Christmas show for the military. At the end, they all sang *Silent Night*. "It's sad, isn't it?" she said.

Typically paradoxical, she said she was going to "punish" me for having neglected her. Why was she flaunting herself in her brief outfit then?

We later went to the Splendid for dinner. There was turkey with paper place mats saying "Christmas Greetings." There was a tree and strings of decorations but it all looked so empty.

Sunday, December 27
Ann and I were supposed to meet in the evening but she came around to my desk and said, "Can I get off the hook tonight?" She wanted to go to a military going-away party. I didn't really care that much but felt somewhat hurt anyway.

Monday, December 28

I left my room at about 10:30, biked to the Meyerkord for French toast and two scrambled eggs. The day is beautiful, almost cloudless. When I got back to my room, Earl was there. He had worked on his black Citroën so now we could drive out of Saigon into the countryside. We ate lunch at USAID, then left Saigon via Tran Hung Dao through Cholon to Route 5A south. The road is paved most of the way but was full of spine-jolting pot holes. We stopped at a Buddhist temple, took some movies and were invited to have tea with the "Head Priest." Earl was fluent in Vietnamese so he did most of the talking for the two of us. The main topic was how it used to be with the French who actually lived here in the colonial days. The priest and his staff, of course, like everyone else, are hoping for peace.

Tuesday, December 29

An urgent notice is passed around HQ warning about possible ambushes of American vehicles:

29 Dec 1970   (MACV SEAL)

OFFICE OF THE ASSISTANT CHIEF OF STAFF FOR CIVIL OPERATIONS AND REVOLUTIONARY DEVELOPMENT SUPPORT

18:30 tonight at Chi Lang and Le Van Duyet
Somewhere along Street 12 students will ambush American vehicle
(Report reliable)

Wednesday, December 30

Ann comes over to my desk a couple of times, but only talks about being sick, nothing about going out. I thought I've avoided her too much. Not that I really want the relationship; I just miss the attention. I felt lonely again as I rode the bike down Cong Ly to the Splendid for dinner. I thought that I'm not going back to her after she says she's been with someone else or I think there's a high probability that she has.

The weather is a bit cool now for Saigon. A blanket is needed at night as the temperature goes down to the low 70's. Termites had been feeding on my bamboo chopsticks and there was nothing much left of them.

Thursday, December 31

Another warning circulated about student unrest:

HEADQUARTERS
UNITED STATES MILITARY ASSISTANCE COMMAND, VIETNAM
APO SAN FRANCISCO 96222

Information was received that at 1500 hrs today 100 students are supposed to hold an Anti-American demonstration at St. Mary's Church (Main Cathedral).

From there they will go to the Palace to see the President. If he refuses to see them they will retaliate by burning US Vehicles and attacking US Servicemen.

signed, X, LTC, USA

Ann comes over to talk to me as I am looking out the window. We talk only in general. I say, "The last day of the year," in a drawn-out way. At this she gets up from sitting on my desk and walks away. "Bye," I say, and as she turns the corner she looks back with a smiling "Bye." At that time I didn't want to ask her out for New Year's Eve – I thought she already had a date. That was the beginning of my regretting having snubbed her.

I bugged out at 4:30 almost intent on just saying the hell with it and spending New Year's Eve at home by myself. But this wasn't too good a prospect, so in an office downstairs on the way out I called Bill. We met at the Continental Palace. We ended up buying a mask and a drum and making idiots of ourselves going from bar to bar banging the drum and singing as loud as we could in our drunken state.

Friday, January 1, 1971

I rode over to Ann's but she was not there so I left a note under her door:

HAPPY NEW YEAR!
I stopped by at 2:30 and you were still out reveling! If you want to go out
for dinner at 6:00 it's okay.

I biked to the docks for a while as that was always a good place to relax and enjoy the thought of travel. I then went home, washed up and cycled over to Ann's just before 6:00. She's in a gray negligee. "What are you all dressed up for?" she says. "I don't know; why are you all *un*dressed?" I riposted. She said that when she got my note she threw it away – that was unusual for her as she usually keeps "nice notes like that." She asks "Do you want to go out to dinner by yourself?" I said simply, "No."

"Do you want me to get dressed?" she says in that rising sweet, seductive tone of hers. "No," I said.

A couple of hours later we bike to *Paprika Restaurant* (136-B Yen Do). On the way she says, "This is something I'll never forget – never! Bicycling out to dinner!"

Saturday, January 2
We received another memo at the office about student demonstrations:

(MACV SEAL/SHIELD)

MACCORDS   Date: 2 Jan 71

Memorandum For: ALL PERSONNEL

Subject: **STUDENT DEMONSTRATIONS/TERRORISM**

Information has just been received that the following activity will take place on 2 Jan:

Students consisting of 4 teams will attempt to throw gasoline and torches on American military vehicles during the period 1500 - 1730 this date on the following streets: Hai Ba Trung, Phan Thanh Gian, and Hong Thap Tu.

In addition to above, 20 to 28 Groups will be working the entire Saigon area.

*ALL PERSONNEL ARE ENCOURAGED TO BE EXTREMELY
CAUTIOUS AND TO KEEP MILITARY VEHICLES IN
SECURED PARKING AREAS AT ALL TIMES.*
(Signed)
Director

The student situation is getting worse. I stayed after work and typed the memo to Kissinger and the letter to the *New York Times*, as I had promised Thanh. I put them in the file of classified documents that are picked up by the courier every day. The return address would simply be: "Headquarters MACV, Saigon."

In the afternoon I ask Ann out but she says she's made plans. I turn around dejectedly and go to my desk. She comes back, touching my arm and says she wishes I had asked sooner. I call her and ask about Sunday morning. Will she come over? She says okay then says, "You come to my place." Later she says, "It'd have to be in the afternoon. I can't tell you why now. It's nothing. There's something I have to do."

Sunday, January 3
She comes over to my room in the morning. "Are you ready to leave? *I* am," she says, then adds, "Are you angry with me?" "Yes," I say in a mock annoyed tone. We went to the Majestic. We hold hands but the relationship isn't easy. The Majestic Hotel, famous in Saigon, had an ad in the papers:

Hotel Majestic 1, Rue Tu-Do, Salles climatisées:
Le PHENIX et le TRIANON, Son restaurant LE VERSAILLES
Repas à partir de 500 V.N.$
Singers and orchestra at the bar.

Monday, January 4

Ann and went to lunch at BOQ-2 by military bus and hitchhiked back but she was kind of bitchy and it didn't turn out very well. I thought I was really tired of her tantrums and her flirting (and probably more) with the military guys.

Thursday, January 7

When I woke up, I suddenly felt tough, strong. I would break off this relationship. The weather was invigorating. I really was pulling out from the doldrums.

Friday, January 8

It is good to have it over, once and for all. I can think a little more clearly and have a little more peace of mind now. Between the almost continuous gastric hurt arise feelings of relief and lustful anticipation of the next affair. A realization that I wasn't seriously involved and that the sex was not really worth all the trouble.

I thought of that good-looking gal I had noticed in Colby's office. I would try to find out her name.

At noon George and I go on his Honda to USAID for lunch. Feel good. Great weather. We both wear sunglasses – easy riders cruising over the streets of Saigon.

Saturday, January 9

Today marks the day I feel glad to be over with the affair. At noon I went with Roger to Tan Son Nhut for lunch. He tells me everything that Ann has told him. Roger thinks she's crazy.

Ann asks me to go with her to change money. She says she's afraid. I tell her to just go in, give the money, take the P and walk out. She does an about face and goes back to her desk. She leaves alone at 4:30.

Sunday, January 10

My day off again. I rode the bike through Cholon and instead of going to the docks I detoured and took a right turn a couple of blocks after the bridge and rode all around the island forming Khanh Hoi, the fourth precinct. Some roads here are hardly ever traveled by foreigners. Some kids called out in surprise, "Ong My" (American man). I was an unusual sight.

Monday, January 11

Ann asks what I'm doing for lunch. I said, "What's this new outburst of friendliness?"

"Can't I be friendly?"

We agree to go to the airport. First we were going to go to the Mass but I said, "Oh, yeah, there's the waiting for the bus."

"That doesn't matter. I won't bitch today. I'm not in a bitchy mood today," she said. We walk to the airport. She had a cheeseburger and I had Chinese soup and club sandwich. I didn't have any P so she had to pay. "I miss you," she said. I replied with the equivalent in Vietnamese of liar, "sao." "That wasn't nice what you said." "I just said 'liar' – that's not so bad."

"It's not really worthwhile continuing our relationship with such a short time left," she said. "Yeah," I said, "That's the way I feel about it."

"That's not how you felt when you wanted me back," she said.

"No, but that's the way I feel about it now," I said firmly, surprising myself. She seemed surprised too but the matter rested there.

Back at HQ, she stopped by and said she was going home and go to bed. I joked, "Another exciting evening in Saigon." At this she said, "What do you do with your evenings here?"

"You mean after the Field Ration Mess?" It was a front, this stilted joking of mine. She remained serious. "Oh, maybe to a movie or something," I said weakly.

The six o'clock bugle signaled the end of another day. She simply got up, said "Goodnight," and walked away. "Goodnight," I echoed unemotionally.

Tuesday, January 12

In the evening I: went with George to the *Nam Phuong* restaurant on Hai Ba Trung. We had chicken salad, two kinds of beef and two 33 beers each. Afterwards we made the round of bars on Hai Ba Trung. In the *Red Horse*, the cashier tells the famous story of a woman beggar who came in the bar with her child. She had been a dancing girl at the *Kim Son* in

Cholon, and was the mistress of a Vietnamese colonel. The colonel's wife found out, then paid a cyclo driver to throw acid in her face.

I cuddled up to one of the "hostesses," then bought her a 500P tea. Later she wanted another but I said, "No can do," whereupon she called me a "cheap Charlie" and "number ten," and so I sent her off.

Thursday, January 14

I now felt the pressure of being alone in Saigon. Earl had been reassigned to Can Tho and had written a letter to me:

The drive down to Can Tho was a drag, six hours in all, but the car held up and performed remarkably well. Biggest delays were a very rutted and potholed stretch for about 20 miles just outside of Vinh Long and two long ferry crossings.

Just wrote a memo today to John Vann (US czar of MR4) requesting permission to live on the economy.

Can Tho thus far is a supreme disappointment as a town. Was expecting quite a bit more than I've seen, for a town of 300,000 people. There's one small compact bar area geared to the military trade which makes Hai Ba Trung in Saigon look like Fifth Avenue by comparison. It appears that zeroing in on some good local material is going to be orders of magnitude harder here than it was in Saigon.

George and I have drinks in the back patio garden of the Continental Palace. "Are you coming to my going away party?" he asked. "Of course," I said.

Earl was gone, George was leaving, and my affair with Ann was ending. It was truly a watershed for me, like nothing I'd been through here before.

CHAPTER 13

Saturday, January 16

It was the evening of George's going away party, held on the villa rooftop patio. It reminded me of earlier days in Saigon where we had watched the flares brightly parachuting down on Viet Cong positions north of Saigon. There was plenty of beer and there was dancing. I hated dancing but managed to find an attractive partner; it was that woman I had seen in Colby's office. I found out that her name was Julie. The beer helped me overcome my inhibitions. We chatted during my faltering attempt at dancing and, later, as the party was breaking up she said, "Can I accompany you to your vehicle?" I explained that my vehicle was a bicycle, but that I lived only a few blocks away. We both laughed as she managed to sit side-saddle on the back fender, and I pedaled the short distance over to Tran Quy Cap. In my room we just sat and talked and drank wine, and nothing happened that first evening – it's always difficult to explain why something happens and why it doesn't on that first encounter. She said she would come over to my place the next morning.

Sunday, January 17

I waited for her until noon and, when she didn't show, cycled over and found her still at the villa. I suggested that we go down to the docks to see the ships. It was an excuse to be together and prepare the way for what we felt would probably happen later.

We took a taxi to the Saigon River pier. "I love docks and ships," I said. "Especially here; there is so much to see, so much to dream about, places to go. It's like the water is an umbilical cord to the rest of the world."

"Look at that boat with eyes painted on both sides of the bow. I suppose that's to ward off evil spirits," she said. "And that beautiful white ship over there." It was amazing that we both loved ships and the sea.

I invited her for dinner at USAID. At the restaurant our personalities merged well over a bottle of red wine. After dinner, we adjourned to the rooftop bar for a nightcap. The vibes rapidly overtook us both. I said simply, "Let's go home." She nodded, adding a redundant verbal "Yes."

Monday, January 18
Julie left at sunrise and went back to the villa to get ready for work. It was tough to part after such a passionate night.

In the evening I went downtown and, as I was about to enter a bar on Tu Do, an American jeep comes flying down the street with a GI firing random shots. A Vietnamese policeman ran out into the street but by then the jeep was too far away.

Tuesday, January 19
As I was leaving work I saw that my bike had a flat tire, so I took the military bus back into town and walked the rest of the way to my room.

Knowing that Julie would be working and wouldn't be at the villa I wrote a note inviting her to my place and took it up to her room. I knocked just to be sure and when I heard nothing, slipped the note under the door.

Tet is rapidly approaching and the sidewalks downtown are jammed with thousands of little stands selling everything from soap to guns. The Chinese are painting their traditional red good-luck banners with large gold characters. These, as well as colorful oriental lunar year calendars, are for sale everywhere. Tet also brings tight security precautions and the number of soldiers on the streets has doubled.

So far no rats in my room but they are nearly everywhere in abundance since the Vietnamese dump their garbage on the street corners. One evening, as I was sitting watching TV in a BOQ downtown, I saw out of the corner of my eye what I thought was a small cat approaching the side of my chair. Fortunately I glanced down just as I was about to pet it and quickly pulled back my hand when I noticed the long, thin tail of a rat.

Wednesday, January 20

In the evening after work Julie came over and we went out to *La Casita*, consuming a bottle and a half of wine with our *fondue*.

The restaurant had its ad in the paper:

LA CASITA
RESTAURANT FRANÇAIS
Ouvert jusqu'au couvre-feu
52, NGUYEN-CONG-TRU - TEL. 90 232

After dinner she said she was tired and would come to my place Sunday.

Sunday, January 24

She comes over late in the morning bringing rosé wine. We consume that as well as my *Pinot Noir* while listening to music on the Australian radio station.

"You are just the type of girl I like," I said as we cuddled. She gently puts her fingers over my lips. "Don't say that," as though the actual saying it would destroy the effect and mood. We are together in my room for most of the day and in the evening we go to the Brink for dinner. It's still light and there is a nice breeze coming in the window.

"I don't like to be alone. I need someone – that's why you and me," she says. Why was she explaining, I wondered.

Monday, January 25

We go to dinner at the Nam Phuong restaurant on Hai Ba Trung. There is "heavy talk," as she calls it, between us. It so often happens that when a woman is falling in love, she claims she wants to opt out of the relationship as a clever way to say she is falling in love. The woman is always "taking the pulse" of a relationship, whereas the man usually just goes blissfully from day to day as long as he gets what he wants.

We buy each other colorful Vietnamese Tet cards at a sidewalk stall and stroll to the Continental Palace where we sit on the terrace sipping our drinks.

"Would you be angry if I didn't spend the night at your place tonight?" she asked. "We would just have to get up again right away." Reluctantly I said, "OK."

Tuesday, January 26

We decide to eat at USAID. I told the taxi driver, "USAID on Le Van Duyet," and he said, "Oh, USAID-1." We laughed at his unexpected knowledge.

After dinner we strolled around the flower market on Nguyen Hue, enjoying the dark evening, and the smell of the flowers. When we went back to my place I realized that she was "up tight" and not in a loving mood. She says she'll talk to herself and that "Next time it will be beautiful." Then she laughed and sang: "I Never Promised You a Rose Garden."

Wednesday, January 27 Tet Holiday

Left work at 6:10, biked home. The whole city was packed with noisy crowds. Thousands of people jammed the streets to overflowing, from the big cathedral all the way down to the waterfront. The QC were arresting some man who was shouting and waving his arms. Several jeeps full of helmeted police with rifles were there with lights blinking. Crowds of people watched.

Wash up and go to the villa by bike. Julie is to cook dinner. We have beef stew, onion soup, rice, Ritz crackers with tube cheese, and beer. It was quite a combo but the main thing was being together.

Friday, January 29

We agreed to meet at the Mass for dinner at 6:30. A Filipino band is playing. After dinner, on the way out, an MP jeep with red lights flashing in the night is parked astride Cach Mang to prevent traffic moving past it. "Wait a minute," I said. "I have to figure out what this is all about." One of the MPs, in helmet and flak jacket, carrying a rifle, jumps out of the jeep and stands feet spread apart, blocking the way. An army jeep trying to get through is stopped. "You can't get through," barks the MP. "There's an EOD (Explosive Ordnance Disposal) team (bomb squad) there and they've found some explosives."

But we walk through anyway and, probably because we are civilians, don't get stopped. We take the first cyclo-mai that came along back to my room. It was always more invigorating going by an open-air cyclo-mai than being shut up in a taxi. "We won't take taxis anymore," she said, looking at me and smiling.

Friday, February 5

For some reason I didn't see her for a few days and she did not answer my phone calls. Was she out of town? I worried that she was breaking off the relationship. I hadn't wanted to go to the villa as it would be even more depressing if she rejected me in person. But this day I couldn't take it any longer so I went to see if she was home.

I rode my bike over to the company villa and just appeared in front of her without saying a word.

She looked up and saw me, smiled warmly and said, "What are you doing here?" as only a lover could say it.

"I missed you, you jerk," I said, smiling happily.

"I missed you too but I couldn't say it."

"I know, I shouldn't have said it either."

Smiling, she said, "I'm happy you stopped by." We agreed to meet the next day.

I rode around Saigon on my bike, happy as a lark. I felt the lifting of a tremendous burden from my shoulders.

Saturday, February 6

At 8:15 I went to meet her at the villa but by 8:45 she hadn't arrived so I put a note under her door:

Julie – I'm at my place.

A little annoyed, I biked home and took a shower. But as soon as I had toweled off and put my old khakis on, she rides up to the door on her bike. She wanted both of us to ride bicycles for a while but I didn't feel like it. So we walk to Dakao to a little café off Dinh Tien Hoang, past Kim's Bar. Cognac each and one "33" for me.

I told her I was going to ride a Vietnamese bus to Dalat by myself. She pouts. We walk back to my place. She says she doesn't think she can stay overnight. I finally get her to say why. It's allegedly because I'm getting to her too much – doesn't want to be with me all the time.

Sunday, February 7

She comes over in the morning at 11, in spite of what she said yesterday. We drink vermouth and listen to music on the radio. We spent the day together, and in the evening we walk over to the *Duy Ban Restaurant*.

Their ad in *The Saigon Post* was a mixture of French and English:

Restaurant Duy Ban, deux étoiles, air conditioned,
81 Dinh Tien Hoang Street Dakao; Special French Food:
CHOU CROUTE D'ALSACE.
Cooking by MAITRE QUEUE BAN, ex-cuisine La Bonne casserole Hanoi.

The next morning she has to get up early to go to work, never a good time after the night's loving.

Tuesday, February 9

At night there are a lot of troops patrolling the streets. They wear flak jackets and carry rifles with fixed bayonets. Also, outgoing artillery picked up a bit. No sweat for us old-timers.

Wednesday, February 10

At Headquarters we received another one of those notices from J-2 that they expect increased enemy activity during the next seven days. This includes rocket and mortar attacks on Saigon.

We meet at 8:30 at my place. She says how involved she is with me but that I don't realize it.

We joke a lot, have some wine. Her cute giggle is back.

Thursday, February 11

I'm sitting in my room in the evening after work and suddenly Julie bursts in the door shouting frantically:

"Someone has told Colby's office that you sent a memo to the *New York Times* about abuses in the Phoenix program, and freeing the students. They are going to come to your office at MACV tomorrow!"

It only took me a second to realize that it must have been Ann who turned me in. I remembered that I had foolishly told her that I was going to write a memo exposing the CIA and Phoenix. She was taking revenge at our breaking up and my seeing someone else.

Julie said, "Did you really send that memo? Why didn't you tell me about it?"

I tell her the whole story about the Phoenix abuses that happened in the field, about Thanh, her brother, and getting the students out of jail. She listened spellbound. At first she said nothing, then "You'll have to get out of here! How will you get out of Saigon? You certainly can't go through Tan Son Nhut."

"I guess Air America is out," I said, surprising myself with a weak chuckle. "I have contact with a friend in a shipping agency. I'll call him and book a freighter out of Saigon. Remember the freighters we always looked at down at the docks?"

She smiled sadly, "Yes."

"While I'm waiting for the ship to come in I'll stay at Earl's in Can Tho. I'll take a Vietnamese bus. They won't spot me there."

She came up to me and we hugged tightly. "We'll see each other before I leave Saigon. I'll come back here before I leave," I said. She smiled, "That's good."

The next morning as I am getting ready she said, "You'd better take this," handing me a small .32 caliber pistol that she took out of her handbag.

I said, "I hope I don't have to use it."

We hugged again and said our goodbyes. With tears in her eyes she said, "I won't come out to the street."

I hailed a passing cyclo and headed down to the huge Saigon bus station crowded with dozens of old, dilapidated buses of all sizes and shapes. Men in shirtsleeves, women in conical hats carrying produce amid sounds of bus motors starting up and exhaust fumes filling the air. Here I was an American carrying my attaché case. I couldn't have looked more out of place.

I searched around and finally found a bus with "Can Tho" on the front. I got on and took a seat in the back where there was more leg room. The bus was full of Vietnamese, no other Westerners. I put the attaché case containing the pistol on the floor under my seat.

As we creep through the congested Saigon traffic a bus employee stands on the running board, holding on with one hand and leaning out, calling the bus's destinations to attract new passengers. This slowed the bus down to a snail's pace – I was getting impatient.

We started out southwest via Tan An. At one stop a man got on the bus, his arms and chest completely taped with large, white bandages. I had heard that grenades can be concealed in this manner so I kept an eye on him and on the Vietnamese around him, to see if they were worried.

There were many partially bombed-out bridges that we had to cross on makeshift wood boards. Vietnamese soldiers in crude shacks guarded each bridge. Potholes were everywhere and my head would bang against the metal roof as the rickety bus loaded down with passengers hit bottom then bounced high up in the air only to descend once more.

At the first branch of the Mekong River the bus drove onto an old ferry boat that looked like it had made thousands of crossings. Reaching the other side, we continued west towards Cai Be, arcing south to Vinh Long where another ferry took us across another branch of the Mekong. Finally, crossing the Song Bassac we arrived in Can Tho, the heart of the Mekong Delta.

We were now in the immense delta where the Mekong, dividing into a thousand arms, becomes rice fields in the former Cochinchina.

In the 19th century the great hope of France was that the Mekong River might prove a water-road and an outlet to the rich districts of southern China via Saigon. But that proved an illusion, and that geographical mystery has been cleared away with the survey and exploration of the river, nearly to its sources, by a French governmental commission.

I scrambled off the bus and began looking for some signs of a US military installation – an American flag flying from a building. Suddenly a Honda came up behind me and the cowboys ripped off my watch, literally; the passenger on the backseat sliding his index finger between the band and my wrist and pulling off the watch. They were gone in a second before I could do anything except shout "HEY!" Some kids came up to me afterwards and said they could get my watch back. I realized that this would not happen and they just wanted to get money from me so I ignored them.

It was strange to be in a city so unfamiliar after I had been for such a long time in Saigon.

I walked through the Can Tho market square alongside the river. Masses of squatting peasants in black pajamas and conical hats were selling fish and vegetables. Steam poured from metal pots.

I spotted an official building down one of the cross streets. It turned out to be an American MP station and from there I phoned Earl and he came and picked me up in his black Citroën.

Next day we went to an army post and took a helicopter with a US major to an outlying hamlet where a young Vietnamese man had been abducted the previous night by the VC. We went with the major as he led a group of Vietnamese soldiers into the brush looking for footprints, but to no avail. Outside the hamlet a so-called "fire arrow," a crude wooden stick inside a circle of brush, pointed in the direction of the most recent enemy incoming fire. In this way the American choppers could see where to fire.

I told Earl about being turned in by Ann and my need to get out of Vietnam secretly. I told him that I had sent the memo. He said that took guts and wondered what the consequences would be. When I told him I was going to leave by freighter he showed me the following clip from the *Vietnam Guardian*:

In South Vietnam Monday, Viet Cong guerrillas fired rocket-propelled grenades at three ocean-going cargo ships moving 23 to 24 miles southeast of Saigon. Only one of the ships was hit and the exploding grenade caused minor damage and wounded one civilian crewman, spokesmen said.

I phoned Julie from the military compound in Can Tho. We agreed to meet at the Majestic Hotel when I returned. I would call her from there when I arrived.

Tuesday, February 16

The trip back to Saigon on antique buses was again a rough, bumpy ride, punctuated with ferry crossings of the Mekong, strange banter with fellow passengers, and food hawkers at the many stops. We finally rolled into Saigon late in the day. I got off as near as I could to the Majestic Hotel.

When I got to the Majestic I called her and a half hour later she arrived. We hugged tightly. "Is your ship here?" she asked.

"Yes she is."

We took a taxi down to the Khanh Hoi docks where we had so often ridden our bikes on Sundays. How different the atmosphere was now. We had an emotional last meal at the dockside stevedore's café within sight of the freighter. We didn't say much, just feeling the sadness and smiling at each other. Suddenly I realized that time was passing and I said, "We better go," as though it was a sentence of death. We boarded the ship and went to my cabin. Our final parting was incredibly emotional – as is only attainable when one person is leaving, possibly forever.

Suddenly there was an increase of activity and noise on the docks and we realized that she had to leave the ship. We climbed down the gangway, walked through the dock area, now so incredibly sad contrasted with the happiness we had felt here in days past, and to Trinh Minh The, the dockside street that leads back to Saigon. A cyclo-mai pulled up and, after a tight, last hug, she climbed in. We looked at each other sadly one more time. I saw the tears running down her soft cheek. With the roar of the cyclo-mai she was gone. We kept waving to each other until we were completely out of sight.

Back in my cabin I fell onto the bed with a feeling of emptiness and terrible finality. Why? Why? The radio was playing "My Sweet Lord." It sounded to me like "My Sweet *Love*." And tears came.

As the big ship slowly followed the tortuous windings of the Saigon River that evening, the twin spires of Saigon's cathedral continued to remain visible above the horizon for more than an hour.

The banks of the river looked as desolate as I felt. The former mangrove jungles had been razed and the flat land now stretched out on either side of us like a scene from Hiroshima. Only a few thatched huts gave any indication of life. I watched the city disappear so gradually behind us and thought of all the people I knew in it – this city, this "everywhere" that was shrinking to a point in space and into my past. It was like leaving the planet Earth behind. Because of the hairpin curves of the river, the city would appear alternately at the bow and at the stern.

It took us several hours to travel the forty-some miles down the Saigon River to the South China Sea. Most of the way I was not allowed on deck because of possible rocketing by the Viet Cong.

In the early morning I awoke after a short sleep, the sights of Saigon still faintly visible in the distance, dropping slowly away under the scrambled reds and pinks of a cruelly-ironic beauty of sunrise.

Time goes on and we cannot stop it. How did the Lamartine poem go? I could only remember a few lines:

The Lake

Always pushed toward new shores,
In the eternal night carried away with no return.
Can we never, on the vast ocean of time,
Drop anchor for just one day?

Alphonse de Lamartine (1790-1869)

In the original French:

Le Lac

Ainsi, toujours poussés vers de nouveaux rivages,
Dans la nuit éternelle emportés sans retour,
Ne pourrons-nous jamais sur l'océan des âges
Jeter l'ancre un seul jour?

On the high seas now. Sadly I feel I have really broken away from Vietnam. On the short-wave radio I could catch the fading 'beep' from AFVN news. When they give the news there's a buildup of music that ends on a high note, a long dash in Morse. It was the only connection I had left with Saigon, with all the people in my world. I wanted to see how long I could retain this thread-like connection. At night I'd tune in and there'd be the crackling static and far-off American voices, the music leading up and then; here it comes, a faint beep, becoming ever more difficult to pick up everyday. My world was falling into the past, getting further away by the hour. Thanh with her bouncing enthusiasm, her shyness – part false, but how much? And Julie. I still pictured the tears on her face. I couldn't bear to think of them making new lives without me.

The ship was making slow progress southwestwards. I contemplated our upcoming arrival in Singapore, having a gin and tonic at the bar of the iconic *Raffles Hotel*, and maybe a letter from Julie. Would I ever see her again? What would happen when my memo reached Kissinger and the *New York Times*?

EPILOGUE

My memo to Kissinger and letter to the *New York Times* on abuses in the Phoenix program eventually reached the United States Congress.

Representative Ogden R. Reid of New York proposed an amendment that would end all US funding for the Phoenix program.

CONGRESSIONAL RECORD-HOUSE,

August 3, 1971

AMENDMENT OFFERED BY MR. REID OF NEW YORK

Mr. REID of New York. Mr. Chairman, I offer an amendment.

The Clerk read as follows:
"My amendment would require that no US funds would be furnished to programs which are characterized by a pattern of assassination or torture or other violations of the Geneva Conventions, to which the United States is a signatory.

"This amendment is prompted primarily by the outrageous abuses which have taken place under the Phoenix program in South Vietnam.

"Mr. Chairman, we have had testimony before the House Subcommittee on Foreign Operations and Government Information last month, from Ambassador William Colby, former Director of CORDS, and from a number of other persons which relate to some activities of Phoenix, which,

in my judgment are violative, at the time they took place, of the Geneva Conventions.

"Ambassador Colby stated that since the beginning of 1968 until May 1971, a total of 20,587 persons have been killed under the Phoenix program.

"At least as shocking as the assassinations, torture, and drumhead incarceration of civilians under the Phoenix program is the fact that in many cases the intelligence is so bad that innocent people are made victims. Yesterday two former military intelligence personnel in Vietnam testified that virtually all information identifying an individual as a VCI is unverifiable and frequently completely unreliable.

"Ambassador Colby admitted this problem. In response to the question, 'Are you certain that we know a member of the VCI from a loyal member of the South Vietnam citizenry?'

"Mr. Colby stated, 'No, I am not.'

"The abuses and inhumaneness perpetrated by the Phoenix program make it imperative that we cease to support it at once and do everything in our power to have the GVN stop the program dead in its tracks. Under Phoenix, civilians identified as VCI have been assassinated without any semblance of judicial process. Torture of detainees during interrogation is another hallmark of the Phoenix program."

The Reid Amendment was, unfortunately, rejected.

And what happened to those student anti-war protesters? After the communist takeover in 1975, the cruel irony was that Vietnamese patriots were still being jailed and tortured. A prominent student leader, languishing for years in prison without any charges being brought against him, wrote a letter to the authorities in "Ho Chi Minh City" demanding that he be brought to trial or he will seek "another way out."

A DIRGE OR LAMENT

An excerpt from a famous poem written in 1784:

Man was made to mourn: A Dirge

Many and sharp the num'rous ills
Inwoven with our frame!
More pointed still we make ourselves
Regret, remorse, and shame!
And man, whose heav'n-erected face
The smiles of love adorn, —
Man's inhumanity to man
Makes countless thousands mourn!

Robert Burns

Sadly, now we must write "countless *millions.*"

Printed in the United States
By Bookmasters